Found in the Wilderness

Kuma's Wild Quest for Truth (or Something Like It)

Constancio K Nakuma

Kindle Direct Publishing

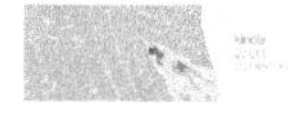

The characters and events portrayed in this book are fictitious. Any similarity to real persons, living or dead, is coincidental and not intended by the author.

ISBN-979-8-9963312-0-8
ISBN-

Cover design by:
Library of Congress Control Number:
Printed in the United States of America

To Jasmine, Jessica, and Julia (aka J-Ladies) for inspiring me to seek truth in parenting. To my beloved Mavis for helping me understand that imperfection is no sin. To my parents, Felicia Uuntaa and Emmanuel Nakuma, for their unconditional love and continued intersession for their extended family. May Kuma's findings bring light to all who seek truth. To the Giver of Life who inspires truth belongs all the glory.

"From everyone who has been given much, much will be demanded; and from the one who has been entrusted with much, much more will be asked." (Luke 12:48; NIV)

Go forth, son, trusting that the protection and blessings of God and the ancestors will accompany you throughout your travels around this world. You have the prayers of the entire village. Remember: the ground you stand on is the only portion of this earth you may claim for yourself and only for the time you stand on it. When you walk away, others may claim it, too. Let no one force you off the ground you stand on. That's where you belong while you stand there.
PARENTAL ADVICE

Introduction

The wilderness had a way of arguing with Kuma without raising its voice.

Here, beneath the thin, obliging shade of a shea tree, the calm was so persistent it bordered on impolite. Every rustle, every breath of hot dry air seemed determined to pull Kuma's attention away from the brutish restlessness of the human world—a world his own kind appeared permanently committed to reorganizing through conflict.

"We humans do seem bent on remaking everything that Nature has provided, don't we? What is it about our humanity that makes us so arrogant as to believe that our imperfection is more perfect than that of Nature?" Kuma bemoaned to no one in particular.

He was called Kuma for short—meaning, *Give Me*—though his full name, Kumayeng, meant *Give Me Wisdom*. At the moment, he would have settled for *clarity*, or at least a bit of *quiet uninterrupted thinking*. Thank goodness, he thought, that places like this still exist. You need time and serenity to think. Humans, increasingly, have neither.

Kuma stared upward through the sparse canopy, his gaze unfocused but intense, the kind worn by people who appear to be looking at something but are actually interrogating the universe. His was not the emptiness of distraction but the fullness of unanswered questions. He spoke again, loudly and sincerely, for an audience he assumed consisted solely of dust and leaves.

"Why can't we have peace? Why is conflict so alluring to humans? Why do we humans feel compelled to remake all of *life* in the image of our own restlessness? Why...?"

"Fo yel ka bong ya?"

The question landed in his ears with the confidence of someone who knew exactly what they had interrupted.

"Huh?!" Kuma yelped, nearly jumping out of his skin.

"Exactly!" replied the voice. "That was my question to you, Mr. Kuma."

Kuma looked down to find Nyeraa the Ant regarding him with the calm curiosity of someone who had been there the whole time and found humans endlessly loud and interrogating.

"Oh," Kuma said sheepishly. "I was just... reminding myself that we humans seem to have lost our way. Wouldn't you agree?"

Nyeraa laughed. A small laugh, but enthusiastic. "He! He! He! he! And how would my tiny ant-self know such a thing, Mr. Kuma?"

And just like that—without ceremony, invitation, or itinerary—Kuma's wilderness quest for truth began, the way all important journeys do: awkwardly, accidentally, and in conversation with someone far smaller who already knew more than he did.

Day One, Stop One: Kuma's Fortuitous Encounter with Nyeraa the Ant

Kuma did not plan to visit Nyeraa. Plans were a human indulgence, and Kuma's desire was to distance himself temporarily from his human kin and habits. This was simply how things happened where Kuma now found himself. Ants, after all, were everywhere—members of the largest extended family in the Animal Kingdom, tiny, tireless, and profoundly sociable. Humans even used them as metaphors. Teaming like ants, they said, without ever asking the ants for permission.

Sensing an opportunity, Kuma seized it with the enthusiasm of a man who had too many questions and no good filters.

"Mr. Ant," he began, "given how extensive your family is, it's astonishing that you rarely fight among yourselves—or with your neighbors. Everywhere we humans encounter you and your kin, you're cooperating, carrying loads far heavier than yourselves. What's your family's secret?"

"Ego," Nyeraa replied instantly. Then paused. "That is—the absence of it."

He motioned for Kuma to lean closer. Kuma complied, much too quickly. Nyeraa stuck a gnathal appendage into Kuma's left ear and whispered conspiratorially:

"Rumor in Antsville has it that you humans are full of it. Ego--filled, I mean. Is that true?"

"Uh... yes," Kuma admitted. He heard a rhetorical question. "But could you help me understand how *ego* causes... well, us?"

Nyeraa sighed. "Please don't make me an expert on humans, Mr. Kuma. Experts require ego. We ants simply couldn't fit it into ourselves. Ego needs one to believe in nonsensical ideas—like the comparative madness of 'I am better than you.' Our formic brains reject such clutter."

"No ant," Nyeraa continued, "can be better than another. Tell me. Do humans truly do this ego-propping comparison thing?"

"Oh, yes," Kuma said cheerfully. "We organize competitions around it. Entire civilizations, really. I was just about to suggest you and I compete to see who can fart the loudest. Just kidding. Mostly."

Kuma paused. "So... are you saying we'd be more united if we abandoned *ego*?"

Nyeraa folded his antennae thoughtfully. "Wherever ego takes hold, the host becomes *egocentric*. Others matter only secondarily. Tell me—would you want to associate with someone who relates to you solely as you being permanently inferior to them?"

Kuma winced.

"Rumor in Antsville," Nyeraa went on, "is that humans think they're superior to all other lifeforms. That's why we Ants keep our distance from your kin. I realize you could crush me easily for bruising your ego—but truth is what you seek, and ants deal only in truth. Long ago, we collectively said: No. Hell no...to ego! Perhaps you humans should try the same."

Lost in thought, Kuma turned to leave. As he did, he noticed a dead locust moving steadily toward Antsville—lifted by dozens of ants, each supporting it with a single leg.

"Unity is strength," they hissed in unison.

Kuma watched silently.

And so ended the first stop of his day's journey—already wiser, slightly humbled, and increasingly suspicious that the smallest creatures in the wilderness knew the biggest truths.

Day One, Stop Two: Kuma's Encounter with Ananse the Spider

Kuma felt it before he saw it: a cool, silken caress across his face—the kind that never arrives with good intentions—just as he turned to leave Antsville.

"A-HA! Gotcha!" chittered Mr. Ananse.

Suspended above him, swinging gently back and forth in his silken hammock—which doubled nicely as a high-efficiency death trap for flies and other winged optimists—Mr. Ananse was glowing with triumph. That glow, however, dimmed almost instantly when he realized there was still no dinner waiting at the bottom of the web. The prey, it turned out, was inconveniently *too big*.

Visibly offended by this betrayal of expectation, Ananse began to hum, then drone, then fully perform Bob Marley & The Wailers' immortal line: "A hungry man… is an angry man!"

Kuma, who Ananse had long ago discovered revered Bob Marley with something approaching spiritual devotion, needed no further clues. This was not background music; it was psychological warfare. "Them Belly Full (But We Hungry)," from Bob Marley's *Natty Dread* album, was a protest against global inequality—and Ananse wielded it expertly. As always, his choice was deliberate: half cultural flex, half grievance announcement, and entirely Ananse.

"Mr. Kuma," groaned Ananse, his voice vibrating through the entire web, "let me guess why you're lurking around here at dusk. Did you honestly believe you could sneak about collecting wisdom from those insect imbeciles without coming to *me*? I overheard your conversation with Mr. Ant, and I wish I could unhear it. Terrible judgment. Just tragic. And this from a *Homo sapiens!* You are definitely *homo*—but the *sapiens* part remains under review!"

"Wow, wow, WOW," Kuma interrupted, rubbing his face free of silk. "Hold on, my dear *friend*, MISTER Ananse. My deeply observant, stealth-lurking, professional eavesdropper of a friend. What kind of friendship is this, exactly?"

"Stealth-lurking? Sneaky?!" Ananse sputtered. "YOU, *Monsieur* Kuma, are the sneaky one!"

"Fine," Kuma sighed. "I'm leaving. But I'll lodge my own protest before I do. 'A hungry mob is an angry mob!' Then again, you wouldn't know much about mobs, would you? You're the loneliest, most grumpy, self-centered, ego-inflated sociopath I've ever met. How dare you posture as a Bob-Marley-style freedom fighter when even your fellow arachnids avoid family gatherings if you're attending?"

"Alright, alright," Ananse snapped. "Mr. Maku—no—Umka—uh—what's the name again?"

"Kuma."

"Yes! Kamu!" Ananse crescendoed. "You win. Now tell me—what are you doing here *really*? And don't lie to me."

"I came," said Kuma quietly, "to seek your wise counsel."

"Oh." Ananse straightened. Preened. Expanded slightly. "Well then," he hissed, visibly flattered. "Stay! Though I generally loathe humans, I shall grant you audience—provided you acknowledge my sagacity. Need I remind you—without boasting—that I am the smartest, wisest, most cunning, amphibious-dwelling being alive? Nook and cranny, hearth and canopy, ground and ceiling—I alone have gone where no human has gone before. In short, I possess all the qualities you humans wish you had monopolized. Minus honesty. And integrity. Trifles."

"...Better than humans, did you say?" Kuma asked softly.

"Yes," Ananse declared. "Better than *you*."

At the words *better than*, Kuma slipped abruptly into a mental freefall. He found himself back in childhood, cross-legged in dust, listening to one of the many Ananse stories told by old Mba Kakyuu—the lanky elder whose joy lay in frequent laughter and the proud display of his toothless gums. One tale rose vividly to the surface.

Once upon a time, Mr. Bader—one of Ananse the Spider's many names—decided he alone deserved all the world's knowledge. He traveled everywhere, picking every brain, small and large, and stored their wisdom in a gourd. His plan was flawless until he attempted to climb the tallest tree, a kapok tree, to hide it—only to discover that clutching a tree while hugging a gourd from the front was impossible.

From the leaves below, Mr. Pontere the Toad croaked, "At your wit's end? Have you tried tying the gourd behind you?"

In that moment, Bader realized that despite having confiscated nearly everything, wisdom had escaped him. Furious, he smashed the gourd, freeing knowledge back to the world.

Mba Kakyuu had paused then, surveyed the children, and explained: "Knowledge is communal; wisdom is personal. Ego suffocates both."

"Humility," Mba Kakyuu had said, "is the path to truth."

The memory snapped back into silence—contemplative silence.

"HELLO! MR. KUMA!" Ananse snapped, waving a leg inches from Kuma's face. "Are you done vacationing in your head?"

"I'm sorry," Kuma said gently. "I'm tired. You're hungry. Neither of us is at our best. Let's regroup tomorrow. Reset your web; I'll head home before night grows dangerous."

Ananse sniffed. The web stilled. And just like that, they parted ways—two creatures burdened by hunger, pride, and the exhausting business of being themselves.

Day 2, Stop One: Kuma's Rendez-vous with Bader the Spider (aka Ananse)

Kuma approached his Rendez-vous with Mr. Bader the way one approaches a wasp nest: slowly, suspiciously, and already regretting it. Dealing with Mr. Bader was never a conversation—it was competitive speaking, a battle of wits. Winning and being right were Bader's twin religions, and his ego could out-arm-wrestle most humans without even stretching. Kuma sighed. Today's verbal duel would require sharpened wits and perhaps divine intervention.

That sense of impending intellectual bruising trailed him as he headed toward Mr. Bader's open-air residence, a place so mobile it resented the word *abode*. As expected—and as fate enjoyed confirming—Bader had moved camp overnight. He might also have changed his name to commemorate the event, because why stop at relocating when you can fully reinvent yourself? Kuma now faced the added challenge of locating a smart absconding arachnoid who was simultaneously nowhere and possibly no longer named Bader.

Calling out "Bader!" would be useless. Mr. Bader never answered to a name he had already discarded. Names, to him, were like old sandals: serviceable for a while, then abandoned without ceremony.

"Well," Kuma muttered, "time to make lemonade with my lemon," lowering himself to the ground and leaning against a shea tree that at least had the decency to stay put. By 9:30 a.m., the tropical heat had begun its daily exercise of sitting heavily on everyone's shoulders. The search ahead promised to be as excruciating as hunting for wild guinea fowl eggs—objects you only find when you are emotionally prepared to never find them, or more commonly, after you have stepped squarely on one.

The Dagaaba will tell you spotting those eggs is impossible because fairies guard them. And fairies, according to reliable hearsay and deeply unreliable sources, have their heels facing forward and their toes pointed backward—ensuring that anyone trying to follow their tracks ends up confidently walking in the wrong direction. Kuma suspected Mr. Bader employed the same strategy.

"But hey—don't take my word for it," Kuma added, raising an imaginary finger in the universal gesture of *responsible skepticism*. "Spotting a fairy is far harder than finding the wild guinea fowl eggs they're supposed to protect. In fact, I've never seen a fairy in my entire life. Not even once. And I've looked—in the way one *looks* while knowing better."

And this soliloquy? Well, it must be Kuma engaging with his unholy trinity of I-Me-and-Myself. Still, Dagaaba folklore insists that when you do find a fairy's footprints pressed into the Sahel sands, the trick is to chase them by running toward the heelprints, not the toes. It is advice both mystical and cruel. It is also—Kuma couldn't help noticing—the exact method required when dealing with Mr. Bader, whose movements, reasoning, and moral compass all appeared to point convincingly in the wrong direction.

As Kuma continued his search—now fully resigned to the fact that it felt less like looking for a Spider and more like negotiating with fate—he remembered yet another of Bader's treasured "fairy-tales." This one was a personal favorite, not because it was enchanting, but because it was so *impressively human*.

Once, Bader had invited three of his Arachnid companions he routinely introduced as his *best friends*—the phrase doing more work than it should have—to accompany him to his father-in-law's village. The mission was noble: help prepare the millet fields just before the rains arrived in May.

The conditions, however, were not.

It was hot. Not "complain politely" hot. It was the kind of heat that made conversation optional and hope negotiable. The footpath wound through rocks that seemed personally invested in the suffering of passersby. The air lay still, unmoving, as if it had clocked out for the day.

Somewhere along this punishing walk, Bader stopped abruptly and announced, "Alright, my friends! When we reach my father-in-law's house, you must remember to call me by my new pseudonym: Yezaa—which, as you know, means *All of you!* I suggest you each pick a name, too, to mark the occasion."

He let that sink in, then continued. "While we're there, I will no longer respond to the name 'Bader.' Repeat after me: Yezaa. Yes. *All of you.* That will be my name for the duration of this visit."

No one argued. Arguing costs energy. They had none.

The truth was, Mr. Bader collected pseudonyms the way others collected regrets. Each new situation deserved a new name, especially if the old one came with inconvenient memories attached. It wasn't that Bader lied more than the average human person—it was that he refused to lose once the lie had left his mouth. Names, to him, were not windows to the soul of their bearer the way some human communities including Kuma's see them. They were emergency exits.

"What was my name on that occasion?" he would demand whenever someone tried to hold him accountable.

And if you answered incorrectly—or honestly—he would smile, relieved. *Case dismissed.*

After six miles of walking beneath a sun that had clearly taken the day personally, the group finally reached the father-in-law's compound. Mother-in-law welcomed them with the kind compassion reserved for people who looked moments away from becoming stories told later.

She handed son-in-law Bader a large calabash filled with water and millet-flour suspension—a drink meant to save all of them from quiet collapse. Bader examined it, then asked, far too carefully, "And who is this water for?"

"For Yezaa, of course," she replied warmly.

Bader looked at his friends, smiling the slow smile of a human person who has just solved a puzzle no one else knew they were playing.

"Well then," he said, "you all heard her. The water is for Yezaa. You will have to wait for yours."

And he drank every drop—unrushed, satisfied, fully present in the moment.

The memory passed, and Kuma realized his legs had forgiven him enough to keep going. He pushed himself upright, using his left hand for support.

Crunch!

His palm sank into dampness. Something slick. Something fragile.

"Oh," he said calmly. "A dozen eggs. Well—eleven and a lesson."

That was how close one could come to wild guinea fowl eggs without "finding" them in the traditional sense.

And just then—drawn by yolk, karma, or habit—"someone" appeared to lick the broken shell clean. He looked exactly like Mr. Bader. But names, as everyone now knew, were a matter best left for formal announcement.

Kuma watched the Bader-looking apparition lick the last trace of yolk from the broken eggshell with professional dedication. The act was oddly domestic—intimate even—and entirely unnecessary, which made it perfectly Baderesque.

"Well," Kuma said, brushing dirt from his palms, "I suppose

this is the part where you announce your name, deny your identity, and accuse *me* of misunderstanding the entire situation."

The apparition paused mid-lick, glanced up, and smiled with a familiar confidence—the kind that suggested agreement without commitment. Then, without a word, he scuttled backward into the underbrush, retreating heels-first in a manner that would have impressed even the fairies.

Kuma nodded to himself.

"Yes," he muttered. "Definitely Mr. Spider. Definitely not worth a second conversation."

He rose carefully this time, scanning the ground as though the wilderness itself might be setting clever traps just for him.

As he dusted off his trousers, Kuma became aware of something subtle but persistent: a rhythmic *nodding* movement. At first, he thought it was his own head, agreeing unconsciously with thoughts he hadn't finished forming. Then he realized the nodding was external.

Near a sun-warmed rock sat Banga the Lizard.

Banga was nodding solemnly—slowly, deliberately—toward an invisible audience that appeared to be applauding him loudly for something that had already happened. Or perhaps something that *had not* happened. Kuma couldn't tell.

Banga nodded again. And again. Each nod carried the satisfaction of a performer acknowledging a standing ovation for some performance no one else had thought to attend.

"Good afternoon," Kuma ventured.

Banga continued nodding.

"To… whom are you nodding?" Kuma asked gently.

Banga froze, then turned, startled, as though he'd been caught accepting praise prematurely.

"Oh!" Banga said, recovering quickly. "Didn't see you there. You must have missed it."

"Missed what?"

"The fall," Banga replied, puffing his throat slightly. "Quite dramatic. Off that rock there." He gestured vaguely. "Could have ended badly. Didn't."

"I see," said Kuma, though he did not. "Was anyone else around?"

Banga looked about, scanning the wilderness with exaggerated concern. "No. But that hardly matters, does it?"

He nodded once more—deeply—toward the empty space.

Kuma smiled despite himself. He had learned, already, that wisdom did not always announce itself in recognizable packaging.

"And" Kuma said carefully, "what lesson did you draw from this… unwitnessed survival?"

Banga straightened. His nodding slowed, evolved, then stopped.

"That," he said, "is precisely the point. If you don't value yourself—if you don't clap for your own survival—who will?"

Kuma felt something settle. Mr. Nyeraa the Ant spoke of unity achieved through banning ego. The Spider obsessed over being better than every lifeform in exactly the same way humans do. And now Banga the Lizard—alone, unrecorded, unvalidated—had introduced an entirely different truth: the need to value oneself.

Kuma sat down. Day Two, he realized, was far from over.

Day 2, Stop 2: Kuma's Extended Visit with Banga the Lizard

Banga the Lizard was still nodding when Kuma sat down. Not hurried nods. Not nervous nods. These were slow, ceremonial nods—the sort bestowed by artists acknowledging applause they had no intention of interrupting. Banga's head dipped once, twice, three times, his eyes half-closed in serene appreciation.

Kuma waited politely.

When the nodding finally subsided, Banga sighed contentedly and turned toward Kuma, startled again to discover an audience that might actually have seen him fall.

"Oh!" he said. "I may already have asked you this, but just to be sure, did you arrive before or after the fall?"

"The… fall?"

"Yes, *that one*," Banga replied, gesturing toward a rock just tall enough to be dangerous but modest enough to feel embarrassed by it. "Clean tumble. Lost my footing. Didn't die." He nodded once more at the empty air. "Very solid performance."

"I see," Kuma said gently. "And… was anyone else here?"

Banga looked around thoughtfully. "No."

"Then who exactly is applauding *you*?"

Banga smiled—a small, private smile. "*I* am."

Kuma felt something in his chest loosen.

"You applaud yourself?" he asked.

"Of course," Banga replied. "If I don't value myself, who will? The rock?" He glanced at it skeptically.

Kuma chuckled despite himself. Mr. Lizard stretched luxuriantly in the sun, clearly pleased to be alive, intact, and adequately appreciated—appreciated by himself.

"I've noticed," Banga continued, "that many creatures wait for witnesses before deciding how they feel about themselves. Very inefficient."

Kuma nodded slowly. Day Two was beginning to show a pattern.

"So," Kuma ventured, "you believe valuing oneself is important?"

"Foundational," Banga corrected. "But easily confused."

He slid closer, his voice warm now, less performative. "Self-worth doesn't shout. It doesn't compare. It doesn't need to be *better than* anyone. It simply says, *I matter.* Then it rests."

Kuma thought of Ananse. The endless boasting. The hunger mistaken for cause for activism with imaginary unjust others...

"And ego?" Kuma asked.

"Oh, ego is noisy low self-esteem clamoring for other people's recognition to pass for self-worth," Banga said kindly. "It's self-value that doesn't believe itself yet. So, it demands confirmation. Constantly."

He tapped his chest lightly. And with another nod, "This"—he paused— "is quieter."

Kuma closed his eyes to recap the lessons learned thus far. Ants banished ego for unity. Spiders weaponized it for dominance. And here sat a lizard who had fallen, survived, and praised himself without ceremony.

"But tell me," Kuma said softly, "how does one learn to value oneself without tipping into ego?"

Banga considered this, then shrugged. "Simple rule. If your self-worth requires someone else to be smaller, quieter, or beneath you—it's ego. If your self-worth lets others stand fully beside you—it's the real thing."

He nodded again—to himself, to the sun, to life continuing.

Kuma smiled. "I think," Kuma said, rising, "you may have saved me from becoming either a spider or an ant."

Banga grinned. "Be a person," he said. "All the way. But gently."

Kuma bowed slightly—a gesture he was learning came easier in the wilderness than among humans. As he walked away, Banga gave one final nod to the empty clearing.

"Well done," he told himself.

And for the first time since leaving the human world, Kuma believed in himself, gently and quietly.

Day 3, Stop One: Kuma Meets Kalingbege the Chameleon, Who Refuses to Pick a Color

Kuma nearly walked past Kalingbege the Chameleon without noticing him.

This was not unusual. The chameleon took great pride in being overlooked. He considered it proof of excellent execution.

"Looking for something?" came a voice from exactly where Kuma had not been looking.

Kuma stopped. Reversed a step. Squinted. A patch of leaves detached itself from the tree and blinked.

"Oh!" Kuma said. "You're… still there."

"Always," replied Kalingbege pleasantly. "Just rarely where you expect."

Kuma laughed. "You startled me."

"That," said Mr. Chameleon, "is what happens when *light* does its job."

Kalingbege shifted subtly. His skin shimmered—not into a color, but *through* colors, like a quiet argument made of patience.

"You see," he continued, "light itself has no color. It is the perfect weaving of all colors. Because of that, it reveals what everything truly is."

Kuma leaned closer, fascinated.

"I don't have a color either," Kalingbege added. "Not a fixed one.

I reflect back what surrounds me. Not because I lack identity, but because I understand perception."

"So, truth," Kuma ventured, "requires light?"

"Precisely," said Kalingbege. "Without light, all things pretend to be the same darkness. With light, each wave reveals itself honestly."

Kuma sat quietly with that. Ants taught unity. Spiders wrestled with ego. Lizards showed self-worth. And now—*light*.

"Truth," Kalingbege concluded, "is not what you insist upon. It is what becomes visible when you stop blocking the light."

Day 3, Stop One Extended: Why Kalingbege Paces Slowly, Carefully, and Without Applause

Kuma stayed.

This pleased Mr. Chameleon greatly, though he did not show it.

"Since you are here," Kalingbege said, "you might as well learn the rest. Light alone is not enough. You must also learn *how* to move within it."

He took a step forward. Then considered it. Then placed his foot down with ceremonial slowness.

"First," Kalingbege said, "learn to blend without disappearing. I change colors to match my environment. This keeps me safe. But no matter the shade, I remain myself. Adaptation is not surrender."

Kuma nodded.

"Your kind," Mr. Chameleon continued gently, "often believes visibility equals value and loudness equals influence. That is... exhausting. Sometimes wisdom waits quietly until it is needed."

Kalingbege's eyes rotated independently now—one scanning the canopy, the other observing Kuma intently.

"Second," Mr. Chameleon said, "always scan. Opportunity rarely announces itself. Threats do not schedule appointments."

Kuma thought of humans waiting to be chosen.

"Third," Kalingbege continued, curling his tail around a branch, "never explore without something to hold onto. My tail allows me to reach uncertain places boldly."

He paused.

"For you, that tail is your community. Your networks. Especially those who share your history and struggle. You rise higher when you lift up one another."

Kuma felt that one land solidly.

"Fourth," Kalingbege said, flicking his tongue once and then restraining it, "do not waste saliva."

Kuma smiled knowingly.

"Speak less than you listen. Promises are sticky things—don't throw them unless you are close enough to keep them."

Mr. Chameleon began to walk. Slowly. Deliberately. Every step contemplated.

"And finally," he said, "never rush wisdom. *Festina lente*—make haste slowly. Decisions ripple farther than you think."

Kuma exhaled.

"Light reveals truth," Kalingbege concluded. "But character is how you move once you see it. Adapt. Observe. Hold on. Listen more than you speak. Serve something larger than yourself."

He paused, then added tenderly, "If you must shine, shine in a way that helps others see."

Kuma bowed—deeper this time. Day Three had given him something rare: clarity without noise. And as he left, Mr. Chameleon faded gently back into his surroundings—unchanged, entirely himself, and fully present *in the light*.

Day 3, Stop 2: Kuma Walks Home with Zenzanga the Bat, Who Once Argued with Creation

By the time Kuma started home, the day had folded itself neatly into darkness.

The kind of darkness that doesn't threaten so much as invite reflection—cool, echoing, and quietly busy with lives that preferred privacy. Kuma walked slower now, his thoughts still glowing faintly from Kalingbege's lesson about *light*.

Then something flew past his head. Fast. Decisive. Purposefully *not* colliding.

"Easy," said a voice above him. "I calculated your skull and rejected it."

Kuma stopped. Looked up. Hanging upside down from a branch was a Bat, wrapped in his wings like a scholar in an academic gown worn incorrectly—but confidently.

"You must be Zenzanga the Bat," Kuma said.

"Guilty," Mr. Bat replied cheerfully. "And unapologetically nocturnal."

They regarded each other—the human upright, the Bat inverted—each certain the other had chosen an unusual orientation.

"Walking home in the dark?" Zenzanga asked.

"I am," Kuma said.

"Good. Darkness is where honesty relaxes," Zenzanga replied. "Daylight is too busy pretending."

He shifted slightly, then sighed. "You know, I wasn't always this comfortable with myself."

Kuma waited. Creatures, he had learned, revealed their truths on their own schedule.

"Once upon a time," Zenzanga began, "God handed out gifts. Bees got buzzes, stings, and honey-making skills so good even butterflies were jealous. Butterflies got colors so loud flowers leaned in. Everybody got something that fit them."

"And you?" Kuma asked.

"I," said Mr. Bat proudly, "I got flight *and* fur. Teeth sharp enough to shatter mosquitoes mid-sentence. Warm blood. Baby pouches. Excellent hearing. Very good package."

He paused.

"Didn't like it."

Kuma smiled gently. This story was already familiar to humans in other shapes.

"So I went to God," Zenzanga continued, "and demanded to be made better-looking."

God, patient but practical, allowed three wishes.

"First, I wanted to look like a mouse. Live in human homes. Cheese. Drama."

God obliged.

"Second, I wanted human food tastes. Sweet, savory, variety."

Granted again.

"And then," Zenzanga said quietly, "I looked at myself."

He shrugged his wings.

"I panicked. I didn't recognize me. So, for my final wish," he said, "I demanded to be exactly who I was in the first place."

Kuma inhaled softly.

"And God?"

Zenzanga chuckled. "God was... unmoved by my indecision. The consequence wasn't fire or brimstone. It was alignment."

"You keep rejecting yourself," God said, "so you will live where appearances matter less. You will hang upside down. You will walk with night. And you will learn."

Zenzanga waved a wing around. "Turns out, night suits me. I fly better. See better. Live better."

He glanced at Kuma, eyes bright.

"But I wasn't grateful at first. No, no. I was bitter."

"Oh dear," Kuma said.

"Oh yes," Zenzanga replied. "I decided to punish God."

Kuma covered his face with one hand.

"I aimed my behind skyward," Zenzanga continued gravely, "and launched my retaliation."

He paused for effect.

"The guano rebelled."

Kuma burst out laughing.

"Mid-flight," Zenzanga said, "it declared it had no quarrel with God, turned around, and came right back to me. One must be careful weaponizing things that have ethics."

They sat together in the dark, laughter dissolving into calm.

"So," Kuma asked, "what did you learn?"

Zenzanga folded his wings close, comfortable in stillness.

"That self-rejection is louder than truth. That gratitude begins when you stop trying to renegotiate your design. And that hiding is unnecessary once you accept the angles you were built with."

He smiled.

"I am not upside down," Zenzanga concluded. "The world just forgets there are other ways to stand."

Kuma bowed his head in thanks. His mind went straight to these questions about humankind prompted by Mr. Bat's reflections: Is our human restlessness a symptom of trying to renegotiate our design? Do we humans walk around disguised in clothing because we have not accepted the angles we were built with?

As Zenzanga dropped silently into the night, Kuma felt something settle—not the absence of light, but its companion.

And for the first time, the road home felt entirely right.

Day 4, Stop 1: Kuma Learns About Self-Help from Eggu the Crocodile, Who Did Not Move an Inch

Morning arrived heavy and warm, like a thought that refused to be hurried.

Kuma walked the well-known path toward the tropical mud pond near his home, still carrying the quiet residue of yesterday's lessons. The air smelled of damp earth, algae, and something less philosophical. Something... committed.

That was when he saw Eggu the Crocodile.

Eggu lay half-submerged at the pond's edge, stretched full length on the bank, basking in the early sun. His mouth was wide open—*unreasonably* wide—as though he had begun a yawn he never intended to finish. He was so still, so convincingly lifeless, Kuma stopped walking.

"Oh no," Kuma whispered. "Not you, too."

Eggu did not respond.

Between Eggu's massive, unflinching jaws lingered fragments of earlier meals—unidentified, decomposing, and passionately aromatic. The stench carried far and wide, announcing opportunity in several dialects of decay.

Flies arrived first.

They swarmed Eggu's mouth eagerly, delighted by what they believed must surely be a free buffet left behind by fate or incompetence. They buzzed joyfully, cackling in the careless way only

Vultures would.

Kuma watched, fascinated and slightly repulsed. Eggu remained still. Painfully still. Minutes passed. Then more. Kuma wondered if crocodiles ever developed jaw cramps.

Once Eggu's mouth was sufficiently crowded with flies, he snapped his jaws shut with a sound that felt final in several metaphysical ways.

Silence.

Eggu swallowed thoughtfully. Then he opened one eye.

"Well," he said, "that was satisfying."

Kuma blinked.

"You're alive!"

"Deeply so," Eggu replied. "I was just working."

Kuma stepped closer. "You didn't move for a very long time."

Eggu inclined his head slightly—an exhausting gesture, clearly undertaken with intention. "Indeed. People misunderstand that part. They think stillness is laziness."

He paused.

"It isn't."

Eggu shifted his weight just enough to remind the pond who was in charge.

"Those flies," he continued calmly, "made a classic mistake. They smelled opportunity and assumed effort was optional."

Kuma nodded slowly.

"They believed in the myth of the free meal," Eggu said, narrowing his eyes. "Only fools think they are the smartest ones who can enjoy without contributing."

"But you," Kuma said, "didn't *do* anything."

Eggu chuckled—a low, wet sound. "Ah. That's where humans get confused." He flips his tail on the miry bank, leaving a deep groove in the muck.

“Keeping one’s mouth open for that long is work. Remaining still when instinct urges movement is work. Risking failure after patience is work.”

Kuma sat down.

“Self-help,” Eggu continued, “often looks like nothing from the outside. That’s why many don’t believe in it. They only respect loud labor.”

He glanced back at the now-empty sky.

“Those flies wanted steak without stake. I provided the lesson.”

Kuma smiled. Ants carried together. Bats accepted themselves. And crocodiles—apparently—waited.

“You humans—maybe not *you*, so, I should say *some* humans” Eggu said gently, “often complain no one helps them. Yet they refuse to place themselves where help can find them. Or they want assistance without effort.”

He closed one eye again, basking.

“Put skin in the game,” Eggu concluded. “Even when the work feels invisible. Especially then. Cutting corners too early only gets you cornered and stuck in life’s quagmire.”

The sun climbed higher. Kuma rosc, bowing slightly.

“Thank you.”

Eggu opened one eye. “For what?”

“For reminding me,” Kuma said, “that patience is also participation.”

Eggu smiled—a stinky and terrifying but sincere expression to behold.

As Kuma walked away, the pond returned to its quiet breathing, and Eggu resumed his stillness—working harder than anyone noticed.

Day 4, Stop 2: Kuma's Visit with Mrs. Kyengkyempelaa the Cattle Egret

Kuma left the mud pond with Eggu's words settling heavily —and productively—in his thoughts. Self-help, patience, stake in the game. He hadn't gone far when the ground itself seemed to come alive.

A slow procession of hooves advanced across the grassland: Mr. Naabo the Bovine and his extended family, grazing with the confident calm of creatures who had never heard of deadlines and did not intend to start now.

Some perched on their sturdy backs and others striding eagerly at their flanks were white flashes of movement—Mrs. Kyengkyempelaa the Cattle Egret and her family, alert, light-footed, and intensely focused.

The two families moved as one unit, from dawn toward wherever lunch happened to be hiding. Mrs. Kyengkyempelaa spotted Kuma and flapped over, landing nearby with impeccable timing.

"You're just in time," she said briskly. "Or very nearly too late."

"For what?" Kuma asked.

"For everything," Kyengkyempelaa replied, already scanning the grass. "I bet you don't remember me now, Kuma?" continued Kyengkyempelaa. "It's been over three score years, I know! And you look a lot more mature now, and should I say wiser, too? You used to be just a child, then, maybe 10 years old?"

As Mr. Bovine's family indulged in their extended brunch, tongues sickling up bales of verdant veggies, insects sprang from the disturbed ground—among them beetles, grasshoppers, and swarmers (aka winged termites)—panicked by the sudden eviction notices issued by hooves. Kyengkyempelaa and her kin snapped them up mid-escape with astonishing precision.

"No standing invitation," Kyengkyempelaa said, swallowing with urgency. "Opportunities move, you know. You can't be too sloppy keeping up."

Kuma watched as a swarmer attempted to fly too late, wings catching the breeze just long enough to betray him.

"Poor timing," Kuma murmured.

"Exactly," said Kyengkyempelaa. "Wings are a privilege, not a security guarantee." She nodded toward Mr. Bovine. "We work together. They don't feed us out of kindness, and we don't clean them out of charity. Everyone shows up and does their part. Commensalism is what we call our relationship. Do you humans practice commensalism?"

Kuma noticed there was no scrambling for position, no arguing over insects, no entitlement.

"Yes, with dogs… sort of," Kuma stuttered, like a school boy surprised with a question while dozing off behind their textbook.

"Not to start any gossip, but to make my point, can you believe that Gyugni the Vulture," Mrs. Kyengkyempelaa continued, "lamented that the reason Vultures don't eat grass, which is free and nutritious food for anyone willing to cut it, is because they hate the amount of work required to cut it? They find chewing to be too much work, too, Mr. Vulture had complained to me. So, they wait. They complain. They accuse the world of injustice. They feed on carrion to avoid chewing. We Egrets consider them lazy. And their laziness speeds up their aging. Can you believe it?"

She snapped up another fleeing morsel.

Kuma was quietly admiring Mrs. Kyengkyempelaa's multitasking dexterity and youthful appearance.

"We don't wait," she said. "We walk with those who move the world. Work is our lifeblood."

Kuma smiled. Ants carried together. Crocodiles waited deliberately. And here—urgency and hard work without panic. Kuma's wisdom was steadily growing.

"And the plumes?" Kuma asked, glancing at Mrs. Egret's elegant feathers and distracted by his own reminiscing over her claim that she remembers him from about three score years ago. Those plumes couldn't possibly be sixty years old, he wondered.

Kyengkyempelaa snorted. "Decorations distracted many of my ancestors. Humans wanted the plume without the bird, the beauty without the work. That nearly exterminated us."

She grew quiet for a moment.

"Urgency," Kyengkyempelaa said softly, "is knowing when to act and doing so decisively. Entitlement is believing action is optional but expecting a guaranteed outcome. We Egrets have no regrets for choosing urgency over entitlement. Our survival depends on it."

Mr. Bovine flicked his tail appreciatively as a young Egret removed an itchy tick from his rump. "Young" might be inaccurate in light of Mrs. Egret's three-score years claim—Kuma self-corrected.

"Collaboration," Kyengkyempelaa concluded, "is recognizing that no one eats alone—not *truly*."

The cattle moved on. Egrets followed in lockstep. Kuma stood watching until the white shapes melted back into motion. Day Four had added other truths:

Show up early. Move with others. Don't expect still grass to feed you. Put in your full share of effort. And befriend work early.

And with that, Kuma turned toward home—just a little quicker than usual—determined to crack the three-score-year puzzle of his alleged encounter with Mrs. Kyengkyempelaa.

Day 4 Nonstop: Kuma's Walk Down Memory Lane in Search of the Egrets

Guinea fowls, chickens, goats, cattle... scorpions and cobras, too. Six years of weekday mini-marathons between home and Duong L.A. Roman Catholic Primary School had trampled most of Kuma's childhood memories flat. What remained sat inside his aging "memory gourd"—a stubborn little vessel that refused to leak entirely.

It played back only fragments, like a scratched vinyl record that had seen both glory and neglect. The same scenes. The same sounds. Saturday and Sunday scenes and sounds only. Everything—except cattle egrets—disc-jockeyed into timeless fossils. And yet, somehow, Kuma knew those egrets had been there.

"Bingo!" Kuma announced to the empty road, startling no one and impressing even fewer. "It's got to be *that day*."

That day had been a Saturday. It might have been a Sunday. Mid-morning. The kind of morning that made you question your loyalty to the sun. He had seen many of those.

The heat had risen with the temper of a provoked puff adder. Not just hot—*Habanero pepper hot*. The sort of heat that made even shadows reconsider their life choices. Trees folded their leaves as if trying to disappear into themselves. Canopies shrank like embarrassed witnesses. The air hung limp, thoroughly defeated. Sunrays did not shine; they attacked—sharp, deliberate, and personal.

That day, Kuma had stepped into that furnace fully equipped for duty—and mild suffering. His cudgel rested on his left shoulder like a badge of authority he had not yet earned. A goat-skin bag ran diagonally across his back, from right shoulder to left waistband, clinging like a co-conspirator. At his right hip dangled his prized possession: a baby-sized water gourd, sloshing gently with whatever hope remained.

He looked, by all accounts, like a fairy who had misplaced his extra thick and knotted natural head gear and found a belly instead. A very determined belly. One that pushed forward as though it had its own itinerary. It bulged with the stubborn confidence of a balloon managed by an overambitious toddler—half-inflated but unwilling to admit defeat. Running, therefore, required strategy. Too much forward enthusiasm, and Kuma would arrive face-first before the rest of him had time to object.

Inside the goat-skin bag was the unmistakable silhouette of a recycled Coca-Cola bottle—Kuma's culinary innovation. Corked with a carefully carved corn cob, the bottle held millet soaking patiently in water. By the unspoken laws of Kuma's world, this counted as cooking. Lunch was not just prepared; it was *being become*.

"Those were the good old days," Kuma muttered, smiling again at no one. "Awe. Innocence. Positivity... and questionable menu planning."

Kuma walked on, slower now, letting memory take the lead. One foot in the present, the other stubbornly wandering the past. And then—they appeared. The cattle egrets. Always punctual. Always composed. Always immaculately dressed in white, as though they had somewhere important to be but chose, out of generosity, to stay.

They perched along the upper beams of the kraal fence like quiet sentinels—lifeguards for creatures that neither swam nor asked for supervision. The deepest body of water around was the pond Eggu the Crocodile called home. No danger of drowning lurked in it for any cattle except if Eggu decided to make lunch out of a gregarious calf.

Beneath the egrets, the cattle reclined and chewed their cod with the philosophical indifference of ancient monks. If they noticed the egrets at all, they gave no sign. No greeting. No complaint. No rent demanded.

The arrangement was flawless.

"How did they even meet?" Kuma wondered aloud. "Was there an introduction? A village elder involved? Or did one just show up and refuse to leave?" He chuckled, enjoying the mystery.

The egrets always rode along, feasting on insects stirred up by the cattle's slow, deliberate march. Exactly like Mrs. Kyengkyempelaa had observed. The cattle, in return, continued their chewing —dignified, uninterrupted, and blissfully unaware of the service rendered upon their backs. A perfect partnership. One ate, the other existed. Both prospered.

Kuma paused, adjusting the strap of his bag as it nudged his shoulder in mild protest.

"Hmm," he said thoughtfully. "That's not too different from Baa the Dog's relationship with humans, is it?"

Baa, he believed, had also entered his life by accident and stayed by strategy. Not quite a servant. Not entirely a friend. Something in between—a mutual arrangement with unclear terms but consistent outcomes.

Commensality, he would later learn to call it. Back then, it simply meant: *we stay, we benefit, and we don't ask too many questions.*

Kuma resumed his walk, his steps guided less by the road and more by the gentle tug of memory's brighter corners.

"Yes," he said, nodding to himself with quiet satisfaction. "It had to be *that day*." And this time, the memory gourd—perhaps out of respect, or maybe just curiosity—allowed the egrets to remain.

Day 4, First Landing Down Memory Lane: Kuma's Early Lessons on Leadership

It was somewhere between the third patch of stubborn grass and the first argument among the cattle that Baa the Dog made her formal entrance into Kuma's recall—though, to be fair, she behaved like she had been there all along and long before Kuma had noticed her companionship *that day*.

Kuma had carefully lifted all the beams off the barricaded kraal gate down to the last two. The cattle exited the kraal lethargically. A left turn was the wrong direction. Kuma attempted what he believed to be a decisive corrective command to the cattle.

"Hey! Get back here!" he barked, swinging his cudgel with an authority that commanded only his own respect.

The cattle paused. Considered. And then, in a rare display of collective disagreement, did absolutely nothing. One of them blinked. Another resumed grazing, slower than before, as though to emphasize the irrelevance of Kuma's leadership style.

Kuma cleared his throat and adjusted his stance.

"Move right," he restated, lowering his voice this time, hoping wisdom might sound more effective when delivered quietly.

Still nothing.

That was when Baa the Dog stepped in. No announcement. No drama. Just motion. She slipped from the shade like a well-thought-out idea—lean, precise, and purposeful. Her ears twitched as though she were receiving instructions from a higher authority that Kuma had not yet been introduced to. Then she circled wide, cutting off the flank of the herd with a confidence that bordered on polite aggression.

A pause. Then movement. Not hurried. Not chaotic. Just... organized. The cattle adjusted. One shifted, then another. A slow ripple passed through the herd, as though a silent memo had been circulated and acknowledged.

Kuma blinked. He had spoken. Nothing had happened. Baa had moved—and everything had happened.

"Well then," Kuma said, recovering quickly, "that is exactly what I was about to suggest."

Baa glanced at him briefly, her expression hovering somewhere between respect, loyalty, and professional deference to an incompetent leader.

From *that day*, the arrangement clarified itself—without discussion, without ceremony. Kuma was the leader. Baa was everything else.

Kuma drew his first leadership lesson: authority is not gained through noise.

At first, Kuma believed leadership authority meant volume. The louder the command, the faster the obedience—or so he had hoped. Baa disagreed. She wasted no energy convincing the cattle. She simply limited their options. A stray cow attempting to wander off would suddenly find Baa already waiting at the destination, as though she had read its thoughts and rejected them in advance.

Kuma noticed. Slowly. Reluctantly. And learned.

"Hm," he said one afternoon, watching Baa redirect a particularly rebellious calf with nothing more than presence.

"So... we don't argue with them."

Baa did not respond. She did not need to.

Kuma also learned that the real work of herding did not happen when things went wrong—it happened before they had a chance to. His second leadership lesson: peparation happens before the crisis.

Baa never walked directly behind the cattle. That, Kuma realized, was the place for those who liked surprises. Instead, she floated along the edges, reading movement, anticipating mischief, adjusting angles. She was everywhere she needed to be—usually before Kuma had even identified that there was the need.

When the herd approached a fork in the dusty path, Kuma would begin to think: *Should they go left? Right? Straight?* Before the thought finished assembling itself, Baa had already made the decision visible. A gentle pressure here. A strategic appearance there. And the herd turned. Not because they had been told. But because the alternative had quietly disappeared.

Kuma scratched his head. "I see," he murmured, though it was not yet clear what, exactly, he saw. What became clear to him, though, was the third lesson: a leader is only as effective as the one who supports him.

By midday, the heat returned with its familiar arrogance. The kind that made even ambition sweat. Kuma sat under the reluctant mercy of a Dawadawa tree (*Parkia biglobosa*) whose leaves had not fully forgiven the sun. He reached into his goat-skin bag and retrieved the Coca-Cola bottle. Lunch had completed its mysterious transformation of becoming. The millet, softened and swollen, greeted him like an old friend who had been immersed in patience.

Baa sat nearby. Not begging. Not demanding. Just present. Watchful. Alert. Waiting—not for food, but for instruction. Kuma chewed slowly, watching Baa in return.

"You know," Kuma said thoughtfully, "if I am the chief herds boy... then you..." He paused, searching for the right term...

though the language of corporate hierarchy had not yet arrived in his village. "...you are the one who makes sure I do not embarrass myself too much."

Baa's tail flicked, once—an acknowledgment, perhaps, or a polite refusal to deny the truth.

"Yes," Kuma continued, warming to his conclusion, "*I* speak. *You* make sense of it. *I* decide. *You* make it work. *I* lead..." He gestured vaguely toward the cattle, who were now arranged in a surprisingly respectable formation. "...and *you* ensure the leadership actually happens."

Baa lay down, satisfied. Not with the praise—she had no use for that—but with the accuracy.

As the sun leaned westward and the shadows began reclaiming their courage, Kuma stood and lifted his cudgel once more.

"Let us proceed," he declared, his tone now tempered with something that resembled humility and understanding.

Baa rose immediately. Position taken. Angles measured. Outcome anticipated.

The cattle moved—not perfectly, not obediently, but steadily, as though guided by an invisible system that had finally been installed.

Kuma walked forward, his steps more deliberate now. Not louder. Not bigger. Just... better paced. Behind him, beside him, and often ahead of him, Baa worked—unseen in her significance, undeniable in her impact. And though Kuma would always be called the herds boy, those who watched closely—especially the cattle, who had no reason to flatter—knew that leadership in that field was a carefully coordinated duet. One provided direction. The other ensured reality cooperated.

Kuma smiled to himself as he walked on, memory and present moment blending into a quiet certainty. "Yes," he said softly, as if confirming a truth long negotiated between observation and pride, “that was the day I began to lead…” He paused, then added with a small, knowing grin: “…and the day Baa began to manage me.”

Day 4, Second Landing Down Memory Lane: The Crisis of the Runaway Opinion

It happened just when Kuma had begun to feel like a leader. Which, as experience would soon confirm, is often the exact moment leadership is tested.

They had been moving steadily across the open stretch beyond the kraal—a place where the land flattened out and gave cattle the dangerous impression that freedom was both available and poorly supervised. The herd was loosely aligned. Not disciplined, but co-operative enough to pass for progress.

Kuma walked behind, chin slightly lifted, cudgel balanced with intentional meaning. Baa was working her usual quiet geometry along the edges. Everything was... acceptable.

Until it wasn't.

A young bull—new to authority and filled with opinions—lifted its head abruptly. Its ears twitched as if it had just remembered an urgent appointment elsewhere. Without consultation, it turned sharply to the right and began moving with the focused confidence of something that believed it had discovered a better plan.

Kuma froze.

The rest of the herd hesitated—as all systems do when a single element begins behaving like a revolutionary slogan. One cow shifted. Another considered. The ripple had begun.

"Oh no," Kuma murmured. "Not today."

For a brief moment, brawn memory took over. "HEY! COME BACK HERE!" he shouted, raising his cudgel and taking three determined steps forward—the traditional approach of noise, urgency, and mild panic.

The young bull accelerated. Naturally. Kuma stopped. He inhaled. He reconnected with brain muscle. He remembered. Then applied the lessons.

He lowered the cudgel. Silence felt strange in the middle of trouble—but also... powerful. Shouting had not moved the bull. It had only confirmed the bull's importance to itself.

"Hmm," Kuma said softly. "You want attention."

The bull continued. But slower now. Kuma turned—not toward the bull, but *toward the space the bull was heading to.* A move straight out of Baa's operational manual. That was new. It was uncomfortable. But intentional.

"Baa!" he called out—not loudly, just enough. Baa was already moving. Of course she was. Baa cut wide—not chasing the bull, but intercepting possibility. Her path curved like a thought that had already solved the problem before it finished being spoken.

Kuma adjusted his position—not behind the herd, but slightly forward and to the left, tightening the space. For the first time, he was not reacting to the cattle. He was shaping their choices.

The bull reached the invisible boundary first. And there—waiting, calm, immovable in intention—stood Baa. No bark. No leap. Just presence. A quiet, undeniable *no*.

The bull paused. Turned its head. Measured the options—left, forward, retreat.

Kuma stepped into view—not aggressively, not hurried. Just... placed. Not louder. Better placed.

The herd held its breath. The system had closed in. The bull blinked. Then, with the reluctant dignity of something that would later pretend this had been its plan all along, it turned back.

The ripple reversed. The herd followed. Order returned—not dramatically, not triumphantly—properly.

Kuma exhaled. Slowly. He glanced at his cudgel, now resting peacefully on his shoulder like a retired argument.

"Well," he said, "that was different."

Baa returned, her pace unhurried, her expression professionally neutral. Kuma nodded at her, adding: "Executive-level work," he said. "Quiet. Efficient. No shouting."

Baa did not smile. But she did not disagree.

As they resumed their movement, something shifted—not in the herd, but in Kuma's understanding of it.

He slowed his steps, letting the pattern become visible: The cattle. The egrets. Baa. Himself.

It had never been a simple hierarchy. Not *leader above followers*. Not *voice over obedience*. It was something else. Something... coordinated. Something collaborative. Kuma stopped walking altogether, watching closely now.

The cattle moved, stirring insects from the grass. The egrets followed—not commanding, not owning—simply benefiting from what movement created. Baa positioned—not controlling every step, but gently shaping what was possible.

And Kuma? Kuma was learning to see. "Ah," he said slowly, the realization settling like shade after heat. "This is not leadership the way I always thought of it..." He paused. "...this is a system." He began counting quietly—not numbers, but relationships: "If the cattle do not move, the insects do not rise. If the insects do not rise, the egrets have no reason to stay. If the egrets leave... nothing changes for the cattle."

He smiled.

"But if Baa disappears..." He watched the edges of the herd loosen slightly—just enough to suggest future trouble. "...everything changes."

He nodded. "And if I disappear..." He hesitated. The system did not collapse. But it drifted. Direction softened. Intent blurred. "Hmm," Kuma said, tilting his head. "So, I am not the system." He tapped his chest gently. "*I* am... the one who must understand it."

He resumed walking, slower now, more observant than before.

"The egrets," he said, "do not lead the cattle. The cattle do not serve the egrets. Baa does not replace me. And I..." he added carefully, "...do not command reality."

He smiled at that. "No. We all *participate*." The word felt correct. Balanced. Respectful. "Yes," he continued, warming to the idea, "the system works because each does what it does well, at the right time, in the right place—without unnecessary noise. Just like Mrs. Cattle Egret had said."

He glanced at Baa. "You anticipate." At the cattle: "You move—eventually." At the egrets: "You observe and benefit." Then, finally, at himself: "And I..." lifting his cudgel slightly, then lowering it again. "...I learn to align it all. I learn what it takes to lead."

The sun softened as the afternoon stretched toward evening. Shadows returned—not boldly yet, but with growing courage. Kuma walked on, his steps no longer chasing control, but arranging consequence. Baa drifted beside him—never quite equal in title, but increasingly equal in influence.

"You know," Kuma said lightly, "if this were a very important organization..." He gestured toward the herd. "...I would still be the leader..." A pause in search of the right word. "...but you would be the one making sure the organization works."

Baa flicked her tail. Agreement—filed, acknowledged, not overstated.

"And the cattle?" Kuma continued. "They are the operation."

A cow sneezed. Kuma nodded solemnly. "Yes. Very operational.

And the egrets..." He looked up at the quiet white observers. "...

they are the unexpected beneficiaries." Another pause. "...perhaps the audit department."

He chuckled at his own cleverness. The egrets did not react. As the kraal came back into view, Kuma felt something settle inside him—not pride, not yet—alignment. Memory had not only returned. It had explained itself.

"Yes," he said, almost in a whisper now, "*that* was the *day*." The day the young bull ran. The day the system held. The day leadership stopped being noise...and became understanding. He glanced at Baa one more time. "And the day," he added softly, with a quiet grin, "my executive assistant saved the entire organization from a very ambitious cow."

Baa walked on. No acknowledgment needed. The system was intact. That was enough.

Day 4, Third Landing Down Memory Lane: Kuma's Lesson on Arrogance in Leadership

It did not happen on a dramatic day. No storm. No rebellion. No ambitious bull announcing independence. Which, Kuma would later admit, was precisely the problem.

"A system rarely breaks when it is loud," he would think much later. *"It breaks when everything looks safe."*

The morning had been almost pleasant. Not cool—simply cooperative. The sun had not yet gathered its full arguments. The cattle moved with a rhythm that suggested agreement, or at least mild resignation. Even the dust behaved itself, rising only when necessary.

Kuma stood taller that day. Not dramatically—but noticeably. His steps carried a quiet confidence, the kind that comes not from mastery, but from recent success. The bull had run the day before. The system had held. And Kuma—Kuma had *understood*. At least, he believed he had.

"Hm," he said, adjusting his goat-skin bag with practiced ease. "This is going well." Baa was already in position. Of course she was.

It began with something small. A drift. A portion of the herd began veering toward a patch of green—too green to be trusted. The kind of green that appears suspiciously healthy in an emerging season of restrained rain. Baa noticed immediately. She slowed. Adjusted her path. Prepared to intercept. Then she looked at Kuma. Not urgently. Not dramatically. Just... a glance. A small, professional communication: *"We may want to address this."*

Kuma saw it. And, for the first time since their partnership had formed— He dismissed it. "I see it," Kuma said. But he did not move. He folded his observation into something new.

Confidence.

"No need," he added lightly. "They will correct themselves."

The Sahel's swarming serpent of heat was already coiling so tightly around everything. Even the scorpions straightened their tails to take a shade break between the crevices of a rock pile. Ahead, a pair of exhausted francolins taking cover under the sparse foliage of an acacia bush buried their heads in the brush—not out of fear, but simply to escape the blinding glare of the mid-morning horizon. From a nearby baobab tree branch, an unimpressed bushbaby used its massive, radiator-like ears to fan itself, sneering at our slow-drifting caravan of cattle, egrets, Baa and me, with the distinct, judgmental air of a local watching a vagrant tourist.

Baa paused.

This was new. Usually, action followed awareness. Today, awareness had been... filed. But deprioritized. Baa held position—just long enough to confirm Kuma's decision. Then, reluctantly, she adjusted—not to lead, but to follow instruction. Or rather... to follow *non-instruction*.

The green patch was not large. But it was *persuasive*. One cow moved closer. Then another. Not rushed. Not rebellious. Just... curious. And enticed by the appetite for a delicious vegetarian meal.

Kuma watched. "They are fine," he assured himself. "We are in control."

A third cow joined. A fourth. The line loosened. The shape softened. The system—still intact—began to blur. Uneasy, Baa shifted again—subtly tightening the edge where she could, compensating without contradicting. But something had changed. The system was no longer aligned.

The ground beneath the green was soft. Not visibly. But sufficiently. The first cow stepped in and sank—just enough to complain. A low, irritated moo. The second cow hesitated—then stepped in anyway. Precisely what a herd does—herding behavior. Because cattle, like decisions, sometimes follow the wrong example with admirable commitment.

Kuma froze. "Ah." The word fell out of him—not as understanding, but as realization too late to prevent it. The soft ground gave way unevenly. Movement became effort. Effort became noise. Noise became confusion. The herd reacted—not intelligently, but collectively. A sideways push. A backward shuffle. A tightening of bodies where space should have remained available.

Baa moved. Quick now. No longer shaping possibility—but mitigating damage. She barked—once, sharp and purposeful. The sound cut through the tension between her and Kuma like a well-placed instruction that had arrived later than it should have. Kuma sprang forward. Now he shouted. Now he ran. Now he raised his cudgel—not in authority, but in urgency. Everything he had learned, he was suddenly abandoning.

"HEY! MOVE! MOVE BACK!" Kuma howled.

The herd resisted—not out of defiance, but confusion. They were no longer choosing. They were reacting.

Baa circled faster, sharper now—restoring edges, reopening space, preventing a full panic. She did not look at Kuma this time. There was no time for confirmation. Only correction. It took longer than it should have. More effort than necessary. More mud splash. More noise. More stress for less progress. A clear leadership failure.

But eventually—the system, bruised but not broken—reassembled. Silence returned slowly. Not peaceful. Corrective. Kuma stood still, beads of sweat, chest rising and falling, cudgel now heavy with irrelevance. The cattle resumed chewing—because cattle always resumed chewing.

Baa returned. Slower now. Measured. Professional again. She sat—not exhausted, not triumphant. Just... present. Waiting. Kuma avoided her gaze at first. Then, reluctantly, he looked.

"You saw that," Kuma said quietly. Baa did not respond. She had always seen.

"I saw it too," he added, as though that still counted for something. A pause. Then, more honestly: "I just... thought I knew better."

The air held the sentence for a moment, examining it. Kuma nodded slowly, accepting what it revealed. "That was not leadership," he said. "No, that was arrogance. Mine."

He exhaled. Then sat down on a small rise, placing the cudgel beside him—not discarded, but reconsidered.

"The system spoke," he continued softly. "And I... overruled it." He glanced toward the patch of deceptive green. "It was not a big problem." He looked back at the herd. "...until I made it one."

Baa lay down in the shade. Close—but not close enough to interfere with his thinking. Exactly where she needed to be. As usual. Kuma smiled faintly, looking towards Baa. "You know," he said, "yesterday, I thought you were my executive assistant." A pause. "I was wrong."

Baa's ear twitched. Kuma nodded. "You are not just ensuring that my decisions work..." He leaned forward slightly. "...you are ensuring that I do not make the wrong ones in the first place." Another pause. "...when I choose to listen. When I choose humility over arrogance."

Baa rested her head on her paws. Kuma's statement had been

recorded. No further comment required. Without further ado, they both understood it was time to head home.

As they rose to move again, Kuma adjusted his position—not ahead of the system, not behind it—but *within* it. More attentive. Less certain. Better aligned. And as the herd shifted back into motion, the lesson settled—firmly this time.

The system had not failed. The system had been ignored.

Kuma walked on, quieter now. Wiser in the way that only small, costly mistakes can afford. "Yes," he said softly. "That was also *the day*." The day he learned that: Understanding a system once...does not mean you get to ignore it later. He glanced at Baa and added, with a restrained grin: "And the day my executive assistant... allowed me to fail just enough to become employable."

Baa stood. Position taken. The system—restored. The lesson—permanent.

The swarming serpent of heat uncoiled its tight loop. The scorpions rearmed their tails in readiness to sting should self-defense require it, as they exited their refuge of rock pile crevices. Francolins scrambled to fill their crops for the night, scratching out the grain crops sown in the sweltering heat of day. And from the peaks of the receded baobab tree came strident cries of agony by what might be a10-day old human infant. That's how those long-legged, massive-radiator-like-eared primates got their "bush baby" name. With the babies crying, Baa and Kuma knew it was time to hurry back home.

Day 5, Stop One: Kuma's Debrief with Baa the Dog

That day down memory lane was 3-score years ago. Kuma relived it with the realism of today. Yelping and canine laughter greeted Kuma from behind the door before he could get himself inside. Baa the Dog was super excited that Kuma was finally home after a very long day of anticipation.

The Baa of Kuma's youth was called Taamengeng, *Self-respect*. Taamengeng answered to her name much like all his human commensals would, albeit nonverbally. Today's Baa of Kuma's current life is called Joy, which would have been *Ng-Maang*, if Joy were fluent in Dagaare. But Joy is linguistically an American pedigree. A monolingual.

Joy could read Kuma's thoughts and diagnose his emotional state with the surgical precision of a human veterinary psychologist. She deployed all canine senses to compose an exact, unmistakable clinical summary. She triangulated the taste of Kuma's bodily sweat licked off his palm, inhaled the odor of fear, anxiety, relief, and lingering philosophical confusion, and captured the visual evidence from his face and every betrayed muscle of his body. In less than a minute, Joy knew what Kuma himself was still trying to admit: the wilderness had not merely tired him out; it had rearranged him.

Joy sat back on her haunches and studied him with the grave courtesy of an elder who had seen many foolish things happen and intended, tonight, to request explanation. Outside, the Sahel evening breathed warm dust through the yard. Somewhere beyond the compound, a goat objected loudly to sunset as if darkness had arrived without proper consultation. A dove cooed with bureaucratic persistence from the neem tree. Inside, however, all authority belonged to Joy.

"Well?" she seemed to ask, tilting her head with that familiar combination of affection, curiosity, and managerial disappointment. "How many creatures corrected you today?"

Kuma laughed, because denial had long since become too expensive. "Enough to qualify as continuing education," he said, lowering himself onto a mat. Joy leapt up beside him with the practiced confidence of someone who had never asked permission for what was already spiritually hers. She pressed her side against his leg and sighed. It was the sigh of a creature prepared to hear the truth, but also prepared to improve it.

"We humans and dogs are remarkable species, aren't we?" Kuma opined, scratching behind Joy's ear. "Remarkable in the way a dust storm is remarkable. Powerful, unnecessary in excess, and somehow always entering the house." Joy thumped her tail once in agreement. If she had words, Kuma knew exactly where she would begin. Why, for instance, do humans give everything a name? Not only themselves. Everything. The dog. The child. The road. The bowl. The room. The land. The seasons. Even storms, and lightning, which come and go without ever stopping to introduce themselves.

Joy's eyes narrowed in the light of the sheabutter-fueled lamp made from a recycled sardine can. Kuma translated faithfully to make this philosophical exchange with Joy accessible to other humans. "You are wondering," he said doting on Joy, "why humans cannot simply *know* a thing and leave it in peace. Why must they label it first, then sort it, then rank it, then argue about whether the label still fits? A dog smells a person and says, 'Ah yes—friend, stranger, trouble, neighbor, one-who-drops-meat, one-who-pretends-not-to-drop-meat, liar...' Efficient. Finished. But humans? Humans need syllables, surnames, titles, prefixes, suffixes, certificates, and if possible, a committee."

He rubbed Joy's neck gently. "I think we name things because we are frightened by how vast life is. Naming is how we hold a corner of the mystery still long enough to feel less lost. We call the river by one name, the child by another, the moon by another still, and then we pretend familiarity has reduced wonder to manageable size. It never does, of course. But it comforts us. Names are our little calabashes for carrying symbolically the nonportable."

Joy considered this with the patience dogs reserve for human explanations that are sincere but clearly underfunded. Then she moved to the next absurdity. Birthdays. Humans celebrate the exact day they entered the world as if they themselves had arranged the logistics. Every year, they gather to commemorate having survived twelve more months of weather, poor judgment, digestive experiments, and each other. They bake cakes, light candles, sing publicly in questionable harmony, and congratulate the honored person for not having died accidentally while learning to *use* existence.

"That one," Kuma said, "is partly gratitude and partly fear with good decorations to disguise it. Humans know, somewhere beneath all our noise, that life is neither owned nor owed to us. So once a year we stop pretending it is ordinary that we are here at all. We feast, we sing, we embarrass one another, and we call it celebration. But underneath the cake and candles is a confession: 'Giver of Life, thank you. We are still here by your grace.' We just prefer to say it with frosting."

Joy's tail swept the mat thoughtfully. "And yet," Kuma interpreted, "we dogs receive life too. The cattle do. The egrets, the bats, the ants, even Bader with all his administrative sins. We all receive breath. We all cling to the morning with appetite. Why then do humans behave as though only *their* arrival deserves annual drumming?"

Kuma smiled. "Because humans are symbol-making creatures. We are forever building little ceremonies around truths too large to hold barehanded. Dogs wag. Birds sing. Cattle return to shade. Humans, unable to wag with sufficient dignity, invent birthdays. It is one of our more harmless vanities."

Then Joy grew still in the way only dogs can: not empty, but listening with her whole body. This, Kuma knew, was the deep question. Why do humans say only they have a spiritual dimension? Why do they speak as though God leaned close to humanity alone, breathed significance into one species, and left the rest of creation as furniture? Dogs do not write theology, but they know devotion. They keep vigil. They grieve. They rejoice in reunion with a purity that would shame many sermons. They receive life, depend on mercy, read invisible realities through scent, rhythm, trust, and presence, and they too stand—each in their own way—before the mystery of the One who gives breath to all living beings.

Kuma exhaled slowly. "My dear Joy, I think humans say these things for several reasons, and not all of them are noble. Part of it is wonder. We are startled by our ability to ask large questions, to imagine eternity, to bury our dead with ceremony, to tell stories about meaning while the millet boils over. We experience conscience, memory, longing, beauty, and terror in forms so noisy that we assume noise is uniqueness. But another part is ego—old, overdressed ego. It is easier to dominate creatures you have first declared spiritually inferior. If you convince yourself that only your own kind reflects the Giver of Life, you can treat the rest of life as backdrop, resource, or footnote."

He looked at Joy, whose eyes held neither argument nor offense—only the steady attention of one who had loved humans long enough to know their contradictions by smell. "Still," Kuma continued, "perhaps the truest thing is not that humans alone bear divine likeness, but that each creature bears divine generosity. Humans may reflect God in one way, dogs in another, ants in another still. The river reflects by flowing. The baobab by enduring. You reflect by loyalty so pure it makes our philosophies look undercooked. We humans mistake difference for hierarchy. Then we call the mistake wisdom."

Now that the serious matter had been sniffed thoroughly, Joy proceeded to the ordinary absurdities of home life. Why do humans close doors and then complain that they feel trapped? Why do they buy soft beds and then sleep crooked at the edge as though apologizing to the mattress? Why do they say "come here" while walking away, "sit down" while standing up, and "good dog" in the same tone they use for babies, grandmothers, and internet routers that have suddenly resumed working? Why do they hide food in cold boxes and then stare into those boxes every five minutes as if repetition might generate goat stew by revelation?

Kuma answered as best he could. Humans close doors because they are forever trying to make private what life keeps proving is shared. They sleep poorly because the mind is the one room they cannot sweep before nightfall. They open the cold box repeatedly because hope, unlike leftovers, rarely stays where it was put. And as for saying "good dog" to machines—well, that is simply evidence that gratitude in humans leaks indiscriminately and often without proper species discipline.

"So why do humans think themselves superior?" Joy finally seemed to ask, settling her chin on Kuma's knee. Outside, the last heat of day loosened its grip on the compound walls. Somewhere a child laughed. Somewhere else, a hen issued final instructions to chicks who had no intention of filing them properly. Kuma looked toward the darkening yard and answered with more tenderness than defense. "Because superiority is the story frightened people tell themselves when they have forgotten kinship. It is the costume insecurity wears to a public event. Humans are gifted, yes—but gifts are not ladders. Consciousness is not a throne. To be capable of naming, building, worshiping, painting, arguing, and writing books does not make us *more alive* than the beings who smell rain before it arrives, navigate by stars, hatch by instinct, migrate by mystery, or love without keeping score."

Joy blinked slowly, which in dog governance is the equivalent of accepting a report while reserving the right to audit it later. Then she licked Kuma's hand once—briefly, ceremonially—as if to say: *Very well. Continue improving the species.* Kuma laughed into the warm Sahel dusk. He had gone into the wilderness looking for truth in strange places, only to return home and find it panting patiently by the door. And as Joy curled beside him, still full of questions about human naming habits, ceremonial cake, household contradictions, and the peculiar human need to stand above what they were meant to live among, Kuma realized Day Five was not ending. It was merely changing rooms.

Day 5, An Extended Conversation with Joy

But Joy, being a serious dog with a deep suspicion of unfinished business, was not done with Kuma. She shifted, turned in a slow circle of emphasis, and settled again with the firmness of one reconvening a committee after discovering the chair had tried to adjourn too early. Outside, the Sahel night had begun laying its cool hand over the compound. Crickets tuned themselves like underpaid musicians. A goat somewhere beyond the fence expressed an opinion so loudly it nearly qualified as policy. Joy lifted her eyes to Kuma and asked, without making a sound, the question that had been waiting behind all the others like a hyena behind a chicken coop.

If humans really believe they alone are made in the image and likeness of the all-loving Giver of Life, Joy wondered, why are they so strangely attracted to fighting one another? Why do they sharpen difference into insult, insult into grievance, grievance into banner, and banner into burial? Why does a creature capable of lullabies also manufacture war songs? Why does the same mouth that prays for mercy become so fluent in contempt before breakfast?

Kuma was quiet for a while. "Because, my dear Joy," he said at last, "humans are both magnificent and deeply in need of improvement. We carry the capacity for love, but also the habit of fear. And fear, when fed bad stories, grows teeth. Many fights do not begin because people love violence. They begin because people are afraid—afraid of losing, losing land, losing face, losing status, losing memory, losing tomorrow, losing the illusion that they are safe. Then ego arrives dressed as righteousness and says, 'Strike first. Dominate. Humiliate. Explain later.' And because humans are excellent at confusing adrenaline with clarity, we often mistake the heat of reaction for the light of truth. And when we realize our self-contradictions, we fall back on overused clichés: 'to err is human,' 'we are imperfect beings,' and such moronic excuses to clear the dissonance. Sorry, your question really triggered me. You smell my frustration, don't you?"

Joy's ears twitched. Her face took on that expression dogs wear when a human explanation contains truth that has not yet passed inspection. "Still," Kuma translated, "how can humans claim divine likeness while behaving in ways that would embarrass an irritated hornet? If the Giver of Life is love, why do so many humans seem determined to become full-time executive assistants to death?"

Kuma nodded sadly. "To say one is made in the image of God is not the same as saying one always resembles what one has been given to reflect. A calabash may be made to carry water and still arrive full of dust. Humans have gifts—imagination, moral memory, language, responsibility—but gifts can be neglected, distorted, even weaponized. We do not become godlike by announcing it. We become more truthful by loving what God loves: life, justice, mercy, neighbor, stranger (of whom there should be none, really), and the troublesome relative who borrows your hoe and returns only the story of why you won't get it back."

But Joy was not finished. She had lived with humans long enough to know that if you scratch one contradiction, three more come out looking for room. What, she wondered next, would humans *not* do for money and power—especially once they have draped greed in religious garment and taught ambition to quote scripture? Why do some invoke God not to serve life, but to sanctify appetite and justify a killing? Why do they bless their own hunger for control and call it destiny?

Kuma groaned softly—the groan of a man who knew the answer and wished he did not. "Money and power are not evil by themselves," he said. "They are tools—dangerous in the hands of the spiritually under-washed. Money can build a clinic or a prison of dependence. Power can protect the weak or become addicted to being obeyed. The trouble begins when humans stop treating God as the Giver of Life and start treating God as a sponsorship label for their cravings. Then religion becomes camouflage. Conscience gets outsourced. Cruelty borrows sacred language, and greed arrives at the village square carrying prayer beads as if holiness were a receipt. Those who make money accumulation their life's purpose are usually the ones who treat God as a sponsorship label for their money-idol worship cravings."

Joy gave him a look that suggested she had seen enough human ceremony to qualify as an unpaid chaplain. She had watched people pray for peace and then insult their neighbors before the tea cooled. She had seen them bless meals they did not share, speak of humility from very tall chairs, and use the phrase "God told me" with the suspicious timing of creatures who had already made up their minds. Dogs, by contrast, rarely invoke the Almighty before stealing meat. They simply accept moral responsibility and keep moving.

"Yes," Kuma said, laughing despite himself. "Humans can be alarmingly creative in baptizing self-interest. We do it because sacred language can make selfishness sound noble and make domination feel ordained. But healthy faith should do the opposite. It should interrupt our vanity, loosen our fists, humble our certainty, and enlarge our compassion. If religion makes a person harder, crueler, greedier, and more delighted by enemies, then whatever else is happening, reverence it is not."

At this point Joy did what all wise dogs eventually do when philosophy becomes too airy: she demanded something chewable. She lifted one paw and set it squarely on Kuma's foot—a formal request for practical content. "Very well," her gaze seemed to say. "Enough diagnosis. If humans are trainable at all, what is your recipe for what they should teach their puppies—the next generation—so they stop rehearsing conflict and begin practicing peace? And please," the paw added, "make it something I can sink my teeth into."

Kuma smiled.

"First, humans must teach children to listen before they are taught to win. Not listening performance. Real listening—the kind that lets another person remain a person while disagreeing with them. Too many young humans inherit conclusions before they inherit curiosity. They are handed enemies before they have met neighbors. Let the next generation hear family stories, yes —but not only stories of 'our innocence' and 'their wickedness.' Teach truthful memory: what happened, who suffered, how fear spread, where pride lied, and how ordinary people paid the price."

"Second, teach peace as a daily household skill, not an emergency slogan. Children learn conflict first at home: how adults disagree, how apologies are offered, how anger is carried, whether power humiliates or protects, whether anyone ever says, 'I was wrong.' If a child grows up watching every disagreement become a wrestling match for dignity, that child will assume domination is normal. But if they see firmness without cruelty, correction without contempt, and consequences without humiliation, they will grow up knowing that strength and gentleness are not enemies."

"Third, stop training children to admire only accumulation. A society that worships money will eventually rent out its conscience. Teach the young that *enough* is a sacred word. Teach them to ask not only, 'How do I get ahead?' but also, 'Who is left behind when I do?' Let them see adults share water in dry season, share credit in good season, and share responsibility in every season. Peace lasts longer where fairness lives. Hungry humiliation is highly combustible."

"Fourth, give the next generation shared work across lines of tribe, class, religion, language, and neighborhood. It is harder to demonize the person with whom you have planted millet, fixed a borehole, shared a meal of shea caterpillars, built a school bench, or carried a sick elder to the medicine man or woman. Shared labor is one of peace's least glamorous miracles. Even ants know that coordinated effort leaves less time for theatrical hatred."

"Fifth, teach religion as humility before mystery, not ownership of God. Let children see that prayer should enlarge compassion, not sharpen arrogance. Let religious leaders self-assess their influence on God's creation not by how loudly they thunder, but by whether the vulnerable become safer near them. Any faith training that produces contempt has mistaken noise for holiness. The next generation must learn that no one honors the Giver of Life by despising those to whom life has also been given."

"Sixth, guard language. Wars are often born in sentences before they are born in street brawls. Teach children to notice when speech turns people into categories, threats, stains, pests, or targets. The mouth is a small kraal from which many stampedes begin. A generation trained to resist and desist from mockery, rumor, dehumanizing jokes, and intoxicating slogans is harder to recruit into cruelty."

Joy absorbed all this with the solemn concentration of a canine considering whether humanity deserved one more chance. Then she yawned—not from boredom, but from the spiritual fatigue that comes from loving a species so gifted at poetry and so vulnerable to nonsense. Finally, she rested her head on Kuma's ankle, which was either canine approval or a formal instruction to begin implementation at dawn. Kuma stroked her side and listened to the Sahel night settle around them: the neem leaves whispering to the gentle Harmattan breeze, the dust cooling, the insects filing their endless reports. Peace, he thought, might begin exactly like this—not as a grand speech from a podium, but as a different way of living close enough to one another to learn restraint, truth, and care before the next generation mistakes shouting for strength. Joy's tail tapped once, as if to say: *Good. Now teach them before breakfast.*

Day 5, Stop Two: Kuma's Visit with Sibiri the Bee, Who Makes Sweetness the Hard Way

By the time Kuma stepped back into the wilderness the next morning, his conversation with his canine companion Joy still reverberated from his sunbaked mudbrick walls. The Sahel sun had already taken up its usual supervisory role —present, unsympathetic, and dressed for overachievement. The Harmattan air shimmered above the earth as if the land itself were reconsidering solidity. Thorn trees stood with the lean endurance of elders who had since long stopped expecting comfort from the weather. Somewhere nearby, a cluster of small wildflowers held their ground in the red dust with the stubborn optimism of people planting sorghum despite a disappointing forecast.

Kuma heard Sibiri before he saw him. Not a grand entrance. No speech. No self-advertisement. Just the joyous hum of somebody gainfully employed. It was the sound of industry without drama, purpose without press release. Kuma looked up and found Sibiri moving from blossom to blossom with such disciplined enthusiasm that even the flowers appeared motivated to reward him. If optimism had grown wings and accepted a very demanding workload, it might have looked like this.

"Mr. Sibiri," Kuma called, shading his eyes, "do you ever rest?"

Sibiri hovered briefly in front of him, wings beating with divinely engineered efficiency. "Of course," he said. "But not in the middle of a sentence the flowers are still speaking." Then, without fuss, he landed on a pale blossom no larger than a forgotten coin and went back to work. Kuma watched, fascinated. Here was a creature who understood that sweetness does not fall from the sky fully bottled. Sibiri gathered it in drops. Minute, painstaking drops. Nectar from one flower. Then another. Then another still. No complaint. No melodrama. No sitting idly on a baobab trunk announcing the injustice of distance.

"You humans say, 'busy bee,' as though busyness were the point," Sibiri continued, collecting nectar with the practiced seriousness of one balancing beauty and logistics. "It is not. We are not busy for vanity. We are diligent for purpose. We gather nectar flower by flower, and in our own bodies we turn what is thin into what can nourish. Honey is love and patience made edible. But while we collect, we also carry pollen from bloom to bloom. So even our feeding becomes service. We do not leave flowers poorer than we found them. We help them become future flowers. That," he added, "is what community-minded work looks like: you return with sweetness, and the place you visited becomes more fruitful because you came."

Kuma looked out over the heat-bent grasses and shook his head in admiration. "And you do all this in *this* weather?" he asked. "Flying these distances? Under a sun that behaves like it has personal grievances?" Sibiri gave the smallest possible shrug, which on a bee looked like a change in punctuation. "The heat is real," he said, "but complaint does not reduce it. The distance is long, but whining does not shorten it. So, we fly. We adjust. We keep working. There is no prize for dramatic suffering. There is only the work, the hive, the flowers, and the sweetness waiting on the far side of effort."

Kuma noticed, too, that there was nothing gloomy about Sibiri's seriousness. He was hardworking, yes—but not sour. There are creatures, and certainly humans, who perform labor as if trying to punish the universe for employing them. Not Sibiri. His industry had brightness in it. "Positivity," Sibiri said, correctly reading Kuma's thought before Kuma had fully assembled it, "is not pretending the world has no thorns. We know thorns. We work among them daily. Positivity is deciding that difficulty will not have the final taste. If the world gives us nectar in droplets, we answer by making honey in abundance."

Kuma studied Sibiri's compact body—sturdy, striped, practical, built more for competence than applause. A bee, if submitted to one of humanity's foolish pageants of beauty, might be dismissed by shallow judges as too small here, too thick there, too busy to pose, too plainly outfitted for modern vanity. No peacock plumes. No butterfly theatrics. No gazelle-length legs. Just a furry little body with a determined face and the aerodynamic urgency of someone late to useful things.

Sibiri seemed amused by Kuma's line of thought. "Yes, yes," he said, "we are not conventionally glamorous. If we waited to feel beautiful by somebody else's standards, the hive would starve and the flowers would hold unnecessary meetings about abandonment. We accept ourselves. Entirely. We do not resent our size, our shape, or our assignment. We are built for what we are called to do. And there is a kind of beauty in being exactly fit for service. What matters is not whether the world calls you elegant before breakfast. What matters is whether your life helps leave sweetness behind at breakfast."

Kuma smiled at that, thinking of Zenzanga the Bat, who had argued with creation and lost magnificently. And Kalingbege the Chameleon, who wore adaptation without self-betrayal. Sibiri the Bee belonged in their company. Another witness against the human obsession with cosmetic legitimacy. Here was a creature who did not spend his days trying to renegotiate his design. He simply inhabited it fully and turned fidelity to self into nourishment for others.

"And do not imagine," Sibiri added, "that I do this alone." He gestured, or rather buzzed suggestively, toward a nearby hive tucked into the secure diplomacy of a hollow branch. "Honey is never the achievement of one inflated résumé. It is communal diligence. Many flights. Many findings. Many returns. Each bee contributes a little, and the little becomes abundance. Humans often wait to do grand things. We bees respect increments. A thousand faithful 'smallnesses' can feed a season."

Kuma nodded, then hesitated. It was not in his nature to avoid the difficult question once it had landed. "There is something else humans say about bees," he admitted. "That you sting." Sibiri turned toward him fully now, not offended, merely precise. "Yes," he said. "We do. But take care how you tell the story."

He settled on a dry twig and spoke with the gravity of one determined to clarify policy after generations of bad publicity. "We do not go about looking for throats to menace. We do not sting because we enjoy hostility. We sting when life is threatened—when the hive is attacked, when our young are endangered, when a giant hand maliciously mistakes our home for a public suggestion box. Defensive force is not the same as belligerent aggression. Self-defense protects what is entrusted to you. Aggression goes hunting for enemies in order to feel important. Know the difference. It is an expensive confusion among humans."

"Besides," Sibiri continued, "stinging is not our hobby. We never do it for game. It costs. We are not careless with costly actions. First there is alertness. Then warning. Then assessment. Then, only if the threat persists and genuine harm is imminent, defense. But some humans skip every earlier step and leap straight to force, then call it strength. It is not strength. Often it is impatience and fear wearing armor."

Kuma felt that settle deep. Sweetness and boundaries. Service and self-respect. Productivity without complaint. Self-acceptance without vanity. Community without performance. Bees, apparently, had built an entire philosophy while humans were still writing mission statements about collaboration and forgetting to bring snacks.

Sibiri rose again and flew into the bright, unyielding Harmattan whirlwind to resume his route among the flowers with no interest in applause. Kuma stood beneath the humming industry of that small, steadfast nation and removed his hat—not from heat this time, but respect. In a world addicted to spectacle, the bee had offered him another kind of greatness: the greatness of joyful effort, accepted design, communal labor, and necessary defense without aggression. As he turned to continue his journey, the wildflowers nodded in the hot and progressively fiercer breeze like village elders approving the lesson. Somewhere behind him, the hive kept humming, busy not for busyness' sake, but because sweetness, it turned out, had to be made on purpose.

Day 5, Stop Three: Kuma's Visit with Pepenaa the Butterfly, Who Insists That Beauty Also Has Work to Do

Kuma had hardly walked a quarter-league away from Sibiri the Bee before the lesson changed clothes.

The Sahel was still hot enough to roast a serious opinion. Dust glowed on the footpath. The thorn scrub kept its usual disciplined silence. Wildflowers that had recently hosted Sibiri's industrial pilgrimage now swayed as if recovering from a well-managed audit. Then, into that practical morning, came Pepenaa the Butterfly—fluttering through the heat with all the unapologetic elegance of a poem arriving at a staff meeting.

Where Sibiri had moved like a disciplined accountant of nectar, Pepenaa moved like delight with wings. She landed on a blossom, lifted, drifted, circled, flashed in the light, and landed again as though beauty itself were conducting field research. Kuma, still humming inwardly with the bee's theology of effort, found himself suspicious on principle. Humans, after all, are too easily impressed by whatever glitters and too quick to dismiss whatever does not obviously produce value. Pepenaa seemed to know this already.

"Go ahead," Pepenaa said, fanning her wings with theatrical patience. "Ask whether I contribute enough to justify the wardrobe."

Kuma coughed. "I was going to be more politically correct than that," he said. "But yes, more or less." Pepenaa laughed—a soft, airy laugh, like dry leaves applauding one another. "You have just come from Sibiri, haven't you? Hard work. Honey. Pollination. No complaints. Very admirable. But tell me, Mr. Kuma: In a world where everything must justify itself by measurable productivity, who will defend joy? Who will speak for beauty? Who will remind your species that existence was not designed only for output, but also for wonder?"

Kuma stood still. This was the trouble with the wilderness: every creature appeared determined to oppose one human excess with another truth. "Aesthetics," Pepenaa continued, "are not laziness wearing bright color. Beauty is one of the ways the Giver of Life keeps creation from becoming a warehouse. Flowers do not bloom only to complete a reproductive task list. Dawn does not paint the horizon because anyone filed a request. Birds do not decorate song with melody merely to satisfy quarterly requirements. The world is not only functional. It is also expressive. And that expression is not accidental. It is part of the genius."

Pepenaa lifted from the blossom and settled on a low acacia twig, where light turned her wings into stained-glass with ambition. "Besides," she said, "if you are looking at me properly, you are looking at transformation. And transformation is one of God's oldest signatures."

She spoke with the calm authority of someone who had been several versions of herself and survived all of them. "I begin as an egg—small, still, unremarkable to the impatient eye. Then caterpillar: appetite with legs and prolegs, devoted almost entirely to growth, chewing leaves with such seriousness one would think I had been hired by famine. Then chrysalis: the holy inconvenience of becoming. No applause. No visible achievement. Just hidden rearrangement. And then butterfly: not a rejection of what came before, but its flowering. Many humans admire the wings and forget the chewing, the waiting, the dissolving, the remaking. But beauty without process is fantasy."

Kuma nodded slowly. Sibiri the Bee had taught him that sweetness must be made on purpose. Pepenaa was now teaching him that beauty, too, is a form of service. Bee and butterfly were not rivals, then. One gathered and built. The other revealed and invited. One said, "Work." The other said, "Do not forget why the work matters." Between them, the flowers had both payroll and poetry. Complementarity humans dismiss on a whim.

Pepenaa dipped one wing, pleased that Kuma's understanding had finally begun to stretch. "And do not imagine," she said, "that transformation belongs to butterflies alone. The Giver of Life is extravagantly fond of continuity hidden inside change. Look closely across creation and you will see familiar patterns wearing different costumes. Eggs. Embryos. Skins. Growth spurts. Ecdysis. Metamorphosis. Shedding. Maturing. Even the creatures that seem most fixed are quietly revising themselves."

"Take humans," Pepenaa continued. "They begin in hiddenness too—cells dividing with the secret confidence of a drumbeat before the dance begins. They are born soft, helpless, and scandalously underprepared, then spend years shedding smaller understandings for larger ones, outgrowing bodies, ideas, and illusions with unequal grace. Toads begin as clusters of jellied eggs clinging onto weeds in stagnant waters. The eggs hatch into tadpoles and become something else entirely, trading gills for lungs and one address for another. Reptiles molt old skin not because they hate themselves, but because growth requires room. Even your own thoughts, Mr. Kuma, are meant to shed when they become too tight."

Kuma looked down at the ground beneath them—the red Sahel earth, laterite cracked in places, patient in others, holding roots, stones, seeds, bones, and memory without filing a complaint. Pepenaa followed his gaze. "Mother Earth herself," she said, "is written in layers of collaboration. Humans extract oil and call it wealth; perhaps they should first tremble and treat it as the deep blood of buried ages. The rock layers stand like her skeletal memory, stacked bones of time carrying the weight of history. The crust is flesh and skin—weathered, scarred, nourishing, exposed.

Trees and grasses are her anchored lifeforms, rooted not in passivity but in purpose, stitching shade to soil, wind to moisture, insect to fruit, fruit to hunger, hunger to motion. The hot depths below, the magma that turns restlessness into continent, and the sea's unfathomed pressures and circulations—these move like hidden regulators, Earth's inward chemistry and slow endocrine wisdom, adjusting what the surface alone could never manage."

Pepenaa rose again and traced a bright loop through the air. "Nothing survives alone," she said. "Not flowers. Not bees. Not butterflies. Not humans. Not baobabs. Not rivers. Not the moon with its borrowed authority over tides. Nature and the wider universe are arranged in complementary configurations, each thing leaning into another for survival and thriving. Light feeds leaves. Leaves feed breath. Breath feeds bodies. Bodies feed labor. Labor feeds community. Death feeds soil. Soil feeds seed. Seed feeds tomorrow. Even distance collaborates with longing, and longing collaborates with movement. The design is not chaos pretending to work out eventually. It is relationship wearing many forms. All lifeforms are built for relationship. Human exceptionalism pretends to be unique in this regard. The rest of us call it the big human lie."

Kuma smiled despite the scale of it all. "So, humans," he said, "should stop acting as though only what can be counted matters?" Pepenaa gave him a look usually reserved for children who ask whether water is wet. "Precisely. Your species is in constant danger of mistaking usefulness for value and productivity for meaning. But a world made only of output would be unbearable. Imagine a Sahel where every flower had been replaced by a spreadsheet, every birdsong outsourced to a memo, every sunset evaluated for economic impact, and every child told not to dance unless the dance improved agricultural yield. Even the termites would stage a protest."

Pepenaa settled one last time on a spray of tiny blossoms, wings opening and closing like a slow blessing. "Tell Sibiri," she said, "that I honor his labor. And tell your fellow humans that I honor theirs too—provided they remember that not all nourishment enters through the mouth. Some enters through the eyes, the imagination, the renewed courage to become. Transformation is not an interruption of life; it is one of life's ways of remaining faithful to its Source. And beauty is not a distraction from survival. It is part of what makes survival worth extending into living a thriving life." Kuma removed his hat again, apparently developing a liturgical habit in the wilderness. Then he walked on through the hot Sahel light, carrying yet another correction to human foolishness: that the world had been made not merely to function, but to flourish—and flourishing, like butterflies, rarely arrives in the same shape in which it began.

As Kuma left Pepenaa behind, still glowing in his mind like a small stained-glass sermon with wings, her lesson on transformation kept tugging at an older memory. Caterpillars, after all, are rarely content to remain punctuation in a larger argument for beauty. They have a way of dragging human memory after them by the sleeve. And so, before Bushbaby could interrupt the evening again with his famously alarming imitation of a human infant in distress, Kuma's mind made one more unscheduled turn into Duong, where Mr. Kakyuu had once converted a harmless squirt of caterpillar spit into a moonlit rescue from almost certain doom.

Day 5, Nonstop Down Memory Lane: Mr. Kakyuu's Shea Caterpillar Hunting Expedition

Kuma slipped down memory lane so suddenly while listening to Pepenaa that he could almost taste the dust of Duong on his tongue again. He was back in the village public square, seated cross-legged beside the heap of retired beams and roof rafters that had long ago resigned from architecture and accepted honorable redeployment as communal benches. There, on those rough timbers polished by generations of elbows, laughter, and gossip, the people of one of Duong's sections, *Laareyiri* (Home of Laughter), gathered nightly to enjoy the company of Mr. Kakyuu—the village's unofficial patron of exaggeration, pun, and survival by storytelling. The mere mention of caterpillar had carried Kuma straight to one of those moonlit nights when Kakyuu, with no teeth but with all the confidence in the world, took center stage to narrate his latest brush with catastrophe.

Watching Kakyuu laugh was already half the performance. His gums flashed in the moonlight like polished calabash, and his shoulders shook long before the punchline arrived, as if his own joy always reached the story first. Children came from every corner of Duong to hear him. They came from compounds smelling of fried Dawada spice and dried onion leaf blend, from courtyards where hens had already tucked their heads beneath their wings, from kitchens where the evening porridge was still giving off steam. In those months when farmwork eased its grip and the moon hung low and attentive above Kakyuu's improv stage,

Kakyuu's stories became a second harvest. His wit was so nimble he could rename peanuts on the spot, turning *sengkãã* into *sẽẽng-kara*— 'uncooked meal'—and leave an entire semicircle of children helpless with laughter.

That particular night was cool by Duong standards—which is to say the air had descended all the way to a temperature worthy of comment and mild theatrics. Children who owned blankets came wearing their family share of one: a strip around the shoulders, a corner over the chest, enough cloth to suggest seriousness if not actual insulation. Duong children understood division without bitterness. One blanket among several siblings was not a problem; it was a system. Above them, the moon laid silver across the packed earth of the square. The neem and wild fig trees stood around the gathering like patient elders. Somewhere in the dark, a donkey protested some unrelated injustice. Fireflies stitched little green arguments into the night air. And from the overhung neem branch the crocking of mosquito bones betrayed the presence of a bat determined to eavesdrop stealthily on Kakyuu's stories.

Kakyuu's reputation had been built on the masterful deployment of words and props. He believed evidence should accompany nonsense whenever possible. So, the children inspected the evening's object with the seriousness of customs officers. It was a *kasogi*, a small oblong wicker cage used for transporting chicks, its opening sealed with a neatly fitted shard of calabash. Such props fueled speculation all day. By sunset, the village had already staged a full pre-story analysis. Was it snakes? Birds? A haunted chicken? Kakyuu let suspense mature properly before speaking. He sat with one hand on the cage and the other resting on his knee like a witness under oath who had absolutely no intention of telling the truth modestly.

Then Kakyuu took them back to the beginning of the rainy season—late May or early June, when the first faithful rains had just softened the laterite and the whole Sahel smelled of wet dust, bruised leaves, and possibility. The shea trees (*Vitellaria paradoxa,* formerly *Butyrospermum parkii*), thick with deep green foliage only days before, had become banquet halls for invading armies of caterpillars. Shea caterpillars (*Cirina butyrospermi*) covered the trunks, branches, leaves, and even the ground between the roots, moving in such numbers that the trees appeared to be wearing living scarves. Everyone in Duong knew them well. Many awaited their annual invasion with culinary gusto. Everyone also knew their habits. This is important, because so did the children listening. They knew perfectly well that the dark spit of a disturbed shea caterpillar was not venom. It stained fingers, yes. It insulted dignity, certainly. But it did not send people to meet their ancestors. Which, naturally, made it ideal material for one of Kakyuu's grander rescues from death.

The shea caterpillars were no minor matter. In the shea belt of the tropics, they were treasured—collected in abundance, steamed, sun-dried, traded in markets, and praised at mealtime with the respect generally reserved for food that appears only when heaven and season agree. People joked, traded songs, and teased one another about who ate what and under which religious technicality. In other words, the village knew both the biology and the appetite involved. Kakyuu had eaten well the night before and, encouraged by this success, resolved at dawn to go and make a respectable caterpillar harvest of his own.

He said he barely slept that night. Whether from excitement or from rehearsing his own courage in advance, no one could say. Before dawn had fully unfolded, while roosters were still negotiating with darkness and the east was only beginning to pale, Kakyuu set out armed with two *kasogri* and enough anticipation to count as a third companion. The village path was cool underfoot, but the landscape already hinted at future severity. The shea trees stood in the half-light like armies waiting to disclose themselves. An owl hooted the night off in preparation for his diurnal slumber, and the roosters, as if in response, cock-a-doodle-doo-d in the day. The horizon glowed with the ominous innocence peculiar to mornings that later become stories. Less than a quarter-league away from his backyard, he met the first great regiment of caterpillars—

and, in Kakyuu's retelling, everything changed at once.

There they were: packed so heavily on one shea tree that the branches sagged like overloaded market donkeys. Kakyuu reached out for the first caterpillar snatch with the casual confidence of a man expecting protein but receiving education instead. The private caterpillar reacted instantly. Touched along the back bristles, it curled with astonishing speed and fired its dark spittle straight at the invader. Now, every child in that moonlit circle knew the spit was harmless. Kakyuu knew they knew. This only encouraged him. He widened his eyes, lowered his voice, and described that black squirt not as a stain but as a launched curse, a venomous arrow, a jet of death so sudden that the whole shea grove darkened, the wind retreated, and the spirits of careless hunters briefly began preparing accommodation.

He demonstrated the moment with full body commitment. Down went the cages. Up flew his arms. Then Kakyuu sprang backward across the square as though reenacting the redemption of a man snatched from the edge of the grave by the urgent intervention of Heaven itself. In his version, danger hung over that shea tree like a black storm cloud with intentions. Every root was a trap. Every branch was an ambush. The earth itself, softened by the first rains, threatened to seize his ankles and deliver him back to the enemy. Yet somehow—by mercy not merit—he escaped. He ran without looking back, he said, because only fools inspect the face of doom while outrunning it. He crossed the yard, burst through his doorway, slammed it shut, and leaned against it breathing like a bellows, newly convinced that the Divine Redeemer had chosen, for reasons beyond all evidence, to preserve him for future storytelling.

By the time he finished, the children were folded over one another, laughing into their borrowed blankets. Not because they believed the caterpillar had nearly killed him, but because they recognized the generous contract Kakyuu had offered them: *You know the truth, I know the truth, and tonight we will enjoy how far a human can run with a truth before it becomes a miracle.* He spoke of the caterpillar as if it had singled him out in personal vendetta. He compared the spit to poison, the shea tree to a battlefield, and his retreat to a holy rescue operation performed at the final lawful second by grace alone. Yet beneath the exaggeration lay something warmly human. Kakyuu was not merely inflating danger; he was amplifying wonder, teaching the children that even ordinary fright, harmless stain, and foolish panic can be turned into communal laughter when retold with mercy. And there in the moon-washed square of Duong, while the Sahel night listened from the trees and the bat eavesdropped from the neem branch, and children wiped tears of laughter from their faces, Kuma learned again that survival is sometimes remembered not by accuracy, but by affection.

Day 5 Winding Down: Kuma's Visit with Gbotol the Bushbaby, Who Sounds Alarmingly Human and Finds That Deeply Instructive

By the time Kuma stepped out of memory and back into the present, the Sahel evening had begun folding itself toward night. The heat was loosening its grip reluctantly, like a touched *mimosa pudica* plant folding up its leaves. Shadows stretched long and thin across the red earth. From the upper reach of a baobab, there came a sound so startlingly familiar that Kuma stopped where he was. It was the cry of a human infant—thin, urgent, indignant, the kind of cry that could summon grandmothers, prayer, and three contradictory opinions in under a minute. But there was no baby. There, clinging to a branch with moon-sized eyes and ears broad enough to fan a cooking fire, sat Gbotol the Bushbaby.

Bushbaby blinked at Kuma with the knowing look of someone long accustomed to getting human attention by causing unnecessary concern in villages. Then he cried again—precisely, expertly, scandalously like a ten-day-old child objecting to the conditions of existence. "You see?" he said at last, as if pointing to evidence in a case already decided. "Even my voice has been designed to remind your species that resemblance is everywhere. The Giver of Life leaves clues all over the place, but humans keep walking past them carrying opinions too heavy to notice wonder."

Kuma laughed despite the eerie accuracy of the demonstration. "It is true," he admitted, "if I had heard that from a nearby compound, I would already be halfway there offering concern and unsolicited advice." Bushbaby twitched one great ear in approval. "Exactly. We share more than humans like to admit. Similar cries. Similar hungers. Similar tenderness toward our young. Similar fear. Similar delight. Yet your kind behaves as though every sign of kinship were an administrative error needing correction." He leaned forward. "Tell me, Mr. Kuma: why does humankind refuse to acknowledge the obvious signs the Giver of Life keeps giving—that all lifeforms were meant to work together, each bringing its strength, each covering another's lack, each helping shape a more harmonious coexistence?"

Kuma rested a hand against the baobab's broad trunk and looked up through its elderly branches. A hornbill crossed the reddening sky like an official seal on the evening. "Because," he said slowly, "humans are brilliant at noticing patterns that flatter us and ignoring those that humble us. We celebrate intelligence when it crowns us, but resist it when it democratizes wonder. If a dog loves, a bat navigates by sound, ants organize, bees cooperate, butterflies transform, and bushbabies cry like infants, then the world begins to look less like a pyramid with humans on top and more like a woven mat where every strand matters. And many humans would rather be a throne than part of a mat."

Bushbaby made a small clicking sound with his tongue—the woodland equivalent of saying, *continue, but improve*. "And what of the mind?" he asked. "Humans keep speaking as though thought belongs to them by monopoly. But many lifeforms have brains, memory, emotion, strategy, attachment, perception, dreamlike states, and the capacity for attention. Why should humans assume that only they can cultivate inwardness, meaning, or spiritual connection with the Giver of Life? Is the mind merely a human brag with shoes on?"

Kuma smiled ruefully. "No, I do not think the mind is a human private club. Brain is flesh, yes—but mind is what begins to happen when life attends to life, when memory gathers, when pattern becomes meaning, when longing reaches beyond appetite. We humans may do this noisily, with books, doctrines, and long meetings. Other creatures may do it more quietly—through instinct refined into trust, through devotion, vigilance, mourning, play, migration, communion, attunement to season and place. I suspect spiritual connection is not proven by vocabulary. It is revealed by responsiveness to the Giver of Life. And responsiveness is abundant in the world, even where speech is not."

Bushbaby's eyes widened with nocturnal seriousness. "Then perhaps the deeper trouble is not ignorance but rebellion wearing sophistication. You remember Zenzanga the Bat and his failed attempt to punish God? Absurd, yes. But was it really so different from humanity's larger project? Have humans not spent ages trying to equal God, sideline God, make God unnecessary, outbuild God, outreason God, outproduce God, and, when all that fails, redefine God into a decorative assistant for human ambition?"

Kuma let out the kind of sigh that belongs to creatures who have accidentally walked into accuracy. "Yes," he said. "That may be the dead end we have run ourselves into. We do not merely want freedom; we want authorship without Source. We want the fruit without the tree, the blessing without dependence, the law without the Lawgiver, wisdom without obedience, creativity without creatureliness. We call it progress when we can finally rearrange life without consultation. Then we look around at the loneliness, violence, ecological damage, spiritual confusion, and exhausted hearts we have produced and wonder why mastery feels so much like exile."

Bushbaby nodded so vigorously his ears seemed briefly tempted to become sails. "Then perhaps humans must learn again how to consult. Not only experts in coats and shoes, though some are useful. I mean consult those of us who remained loyal, in our various ways, to the patterns of the Giver of Life. Consult the ant about cooperation, the egret about timing, the bee about service, the butterfly about transformation, the dog about loyalty, the bat about self-acceptance, the crocodile about patience, the chameleon about light and adaptation. Creation has not been silent. Humans have simply been conducting meetings too loudly to hear it."

Kuma laughed, because Bushbaby had described humanity with painful administrative precision. "Perhaps that is the beginning of truth," he said. "Humility enough to admit that being human does not mean being self-explaining. We were meant to live among life, not above it. To learn from difference, not weaponize it. To bring our strengths—language, reflection, planning, art, moral imagination—into collaboration with the strengths of others, not into domination over them. A harmonious world is not one in which every creature becomes human. It is one in which each becomes more faithfully itself and offers that self for the good of the whole."

Bushbaby cried once more into the deepening dusk, and again the sound pierced the baobab crowns like a misplaced human infancy. Somewhere in the village a woman paused, listening. Somewhere a dog barked back out of professional concern. The evening wind moved through the dry grasses, and the first stars began filing their quiet objections to human arrogance across the sky. Kuma bowed his head toward the small night-watchman above him. Bushbaby had given him no new technology, no policy brief, no strategic framework with diagrams—only a sharper reminder that truth was still distributed generously among the creatures. And as Kuma turned toward home under the dimming Sahel light, he carried with him another difficult kindness: that if humans hoped to find their way out of the dead end of self-importance, they might have to start by listening to those who had never stopped crying the truth into the trees.

Day 6, Stop One: Kuma's Morning Dialogue with Kɔlaa the Cat, Who Defends Independence with Professional Elegance

Kuma was back home to spend the night, and by dawn the compound had resumed its usual committee of noises. A rooster behind the neighbor's wall was conducting unauthorized declarations of victory over darkness. A dove in the neem tree cooed like a clerk reading minutes no one had approved. The Sahel morning came in layers: cool dust first, then pale gold light across the yard, then the rising promise that by midday the heat would again sit on everything with managerial entitlement. Inside, however, the first official business of the day was neither prayer nor tea. It was Kɔlaa.

She was already waiting by her bowl with the posture of a magistrate reviewing a delayed filing. Kɔlaa did not meow so much as issue brief constitutional reminders. Her tail curled around her paws with deliberate displeasure. Her eyes held that ancient feline expression which says, with unnerving efficiency, *I permit this arrangement, but let history record that I noticed the delay.* Kuma bent to feed her, and Kɔlaa began eating with the focused dignity of a creature who believed gratitude was best expressed through continued patronage rather than performance.

Kuma watched her for a moment, still carrying last evening's conversation with Bushbaby in his mind. Bushbaby had spoken from the baobab—wild, nocturnal, uncoached by furniture. Kɔlaa, by contrast, lived with humans. So did Baa. And creatures who live with humans, Kuma reflected, begin to acquire certain human habits the way cooking pots acquire smoke. Dogs pick up our alarms, our loyalties, our territorial speeches, sometimes even our unnecessary feuds. Cats, living among us with their own intact opinions, learn our negotiations, our selective cooperation, our talent for wanting relationship without surrendering control. Commensality, it turned out, was not morally neutral. Live long enough with humans and even noble creatures risk becoming slightly administrative.

Kɔlaa paused between bites and looked up with the cool attention of someone who had prepared a question during the night and intended to serve it before breakfast. Kuma knew that look. He translated immediately. "You are wondering," he said, "why humans compare university professors to cats." Kɔlaa blinked once, approving the accuracy. "Yes," Kuma continued on her behalf, "why do humans say professors are cat-like because they insist on the freedom to think as they see fit? Why is academic independence praised when done in gowns and committee meetings, but treated as insubordination when done with whiskers?"

Kuma laughed softly. "Because humans enjoy independence most when it resembles themselves. A professor refusing shallow conformity is called brilliant, rigorous, difficult in a distinguished way. A cat refusing shallow conformity is called aloof, stubborn, and in need of attitude adjustment. The behavior is not the problem; the species is. Humans are unusually comfortable with freedom when they can issue it as a credential. When freedom comes with claws, silence, and an unwillingness to be summoned merely because someone has made a noise with their mouth, they begin calling it a personality defect."

Kɔlaa resumed eating, though now with the sharpened rhythm of a thinker loading the next objection. "And another thing," Kuma interpreted. "How would humans feel if cats turned their own expression back on them? They say organizing chaos is 'like herding cats.' But what if cats began saying some tasks were 'like managing humans'—all noise, competing egos, unnecessary instructions, and one individual in every group convinced they are the natural leader because they have eyebrows?"

"Frankly," Kuma said, "the phrase would improve by reversal. Herding humans is a terrible assignment. One human wants freedom, another wants control, a third wants snacks before commitment, and a fourth keeps mistaking volume for leadership. At least cats are honest. They do not pretend enthusiasm for a plan they have no intention of following. Humans, on the other hand, attend meetings, nod solemnly, and then sabotage the outcome from the comfort of private opinion. If cats ever adopt the phrase, I hope they use it with precision."

Kɔlaa licked one paw and drew it over her ear with judicial calm. Kuma noticed again what Bushbaby had not carried: domestic influence. Wild creatures tend to remain faithful to their ecological vocation. But cats and dogs, sharing compounds and couches with humans, often begin imitating the household theology. A dog in a quarrelsome home learns suspicion. A cat in a control-loving home perfects strategic noncompliance. Human belligerence has apprentices. So does our failure to collaborate. Baa had learned, through discipline and devotion, to turn human partnership toward service. Kɔlaa, by contrast, had learned to observe the same species and conclude—correctly, Kuma suspected—that boundaries are sometimes the holiest form of self-respect available indoors.

At that moment Baa wandered in, tail moving with the generous diplomacy of someone prepared to love all parties even when one of them shed on his blanket and the other judged his table manners. He sat near the doorway, glanced from Kɔlaa to Kuma, and instantly understood that philosophy was underway. Baa had the good sense not to interrupt directly. He simply exhaled the long-suffering breath of a creature who had spent years helping humans and expected very little institutional reform in return.

Kɔlaa finished eating, sat back, and fixed Kuma with the expression of a scholar who has withheld the central question until the room became quiet enough to deserve it. "Why," Kuma translated, "is independence acceptable when pursued by humans but suspicious when cats insist on it too? When a human says, 'I need space, autonomy, room to think, freedom to choose my commitments,' society calls it maturity, ambition, or self-actualization. When a cat says the same thing by declining to come when summoned, not tolerating involuntary affection, and refusing to attend every emotional emergency in the household, suddenly it is arrogance."

Kuma nodded. "Because many humans confuse freedom with exemption. Especially in highly individualistic societies, children are too often trained to hear 'freedom' as 'I can do whatever I want.' It is a toddler definition wearing adult shoes. Real freedom is not the absence of limits; it is the capacity to choose the good within them. But a society that constantly tells its young selves, 'Be yourself, chase your dream, no one can tell you what to do,' and then acts shocked when it discovers that traffic laws, social consequences, and the existence of other people, planted a very discordant and confused garden, we must wonder how mature that society itself is."

Baa thumped his tail once, requesting recognition. Kuma obliged. "Baa would like it noted," he interpreted, "that some of the societies most devoted to praising individual freedom are also among the least forgiving when an individual goes afoul of the law. They celebrate self-expression all the way to the courthouse steps, then rediscover order with astonishing speed. 'Be uniquely yourself,' they say—right up until your uniqueness collides with property, public safety, tax codes, or neighborhood peace. Then suddenly freedom develops footnotes, subclauses, and a police report."

Kɔlaa seemed pleased that Baa had finally contributed something worthy of the room. Kuma, encouraged, went on: "That contradiction exists because freedom severed from responsibility becomes expensive for everyone else. No society can survive on appetite alone. The road needs shared rules. The market needs trust. The household needs restraint. The field needs turn-taking. The village needs memory. The law, at its best, is simply society's way of saying: 'Your life matters, but it is not the only life here.' Cats understand this better than many ideologues. Kɔlaa does not reject relationship. She rejects manipulation disguised as intimacy."

Kuma leaned back against the wall while the morning light widened across the floor and the compound slowly filled with the ordinary noises of life beginning again: a broom against packed earth, a child calling for a missing sandal, guinea fowl gossiping beyond the fence, the sun climbing toward another unapologetic day. "Perhaps the truest freedom available to creatures like us," he said at last, "is what might be called constrained dependency. We depend on one another, on place, on law, on mercy, on limits, on the Giver of Life. We are constrained, yes—but not merely trapped. Properly understood, those constraints make trust possible. And dependency, when directed toward something greater than the self, becomes the road to a deeper kind of freedom. You become freer not by escaping all obligation, but by giving yourself to what enlarges life: truth, justice, love, responsibility, neighborliness, the common good. That is why the only freedom worth having is freedom *for* something larger than personal appetite."

Kɔlaa considered this with the grave composure of a creature who had never once confused dependence with surrender. Then she stood, stretched from whiskers to tail in one long ribbon of unapologetic feline theology, and walked away—not in disagreement, but in demonstration. Baa watched her go and huffed softly, as if to say that some beings close a meeting by drafting resolutions and others by leaving the room before anyone can assign extra duties. Kuma laughed. Bushbaby had cried truth from the baobab. Kɔlaa had now purred, questioned, and half-dismissed it from the breakfast corner. Between the wild and the domestic, the wilderness and the house, he was beginning to see that harmony would require both loyalty and liberty, both boundary and belonging, both service and self-command. Outside, the Sahel morning brightened over the yard with all the confidence of a story not remotely finished.

Kuma stood in the doorway a moment after Kɔlaa and Baa dispersed, feeling the house settle behind him like a thought that had said its piece. The morning outside was already brightening with Sahel confidence. A pair of guinea fowl ran across the yard as if late to an appointment. Beyond the compound wall, the grass shimmered under a sun still polite enough to negotiate. He tightened his sandals, offered the domestic republic a respectful farewell, and set back out toward the wilderness—where truths tended to move slower, speak stranger, and arrive wearing shells, wings, or suspiciously improved expressions.

Day 6, Stop Two: Kuma's Visit with Kuri the Tortoise, Who No Longer Climbs Trees but Still Rises in Faith

The wilderness received him with the measured dignity of an elder who preferred fewer announcements and better questions. Heat already gathered in the grasses, though the morning still kept a thin shawl of coolness in the shade of thorn and shea. A francolin muttered from somewhere under scrub. Dust lay over the footpath like fine sorghum flour waiting for a hand to make something of it. Kuma had not gone far before he saw what at first appeared to be a patient lightly domed gray rock aspiring to gain mobility. A blink from the rock dispelled Kuma's nascent speculation. It was Kuri the Tortoise.

"Ah," Kuma said, slowing at once, "Mr. Kuri." Kuri lifted his head with the unhurried composure of mobile inertia to whom haste had long ago apologized. "Yes," he replied. "Still alive. Still shelled. Still home alone. Still not accepting motivational speeches from squirrels."

Kuma laughed and crouched beside him. "I have heard things about your community," he said. "Ancient things. Suspiciously vertical things." Kuri nodded. "You have heard correctly. There was a time—long before your species began overproducing opinions—when my ancestors climbed tall trees. Proper trees. I mean serious trees. Not these little shrubs humans call ambition. We climbed heights that would give modern tortoises palpitations just from listening to the descriptions."

He turned slightly, as if aligning himself with an old memory stored somewhere beneath his shell. "Then came the fall. One ancestor—brave, overconfident, or perhaps merely distracted by fruit—lost his grip high above the ground. Down he came through branches, air, and regret. When he struck the earth, his shell shattered into thirteen pieces." Kuri paused for effect, which tortoises do with more authority than most preachers. "Thirteen," he repeated. "Not twelve. Not fourteen. Thirteen. Enough pieces to ruin a family's week and permanently end tree-climbing as a testudinal cultural hobby."

Kuma's smile softened. Kuri's voice did too. "They left him for dead," he said. "And to be fair, the evidence supported that conclusion. Shell broken. Breath thin. Dust gathering. Vultures already filing optimistic paperwork from a nearby branch to dispose of his carcass. But the Giver of Life was not done. What no shell could hold together, only grace could. What looked finished was only interrupted. Bit by bit, bone by bone, breath by breath, healing came. Not by noise. Not by swagger. By mercy alone. By intervention. By the quiet power of the One who can mend what creatures have already buried in their minds."

Kuri lifted his chin with modest pride. "That is why we carry the story in our shells and why I carry it in my mouth. I was healed —my people were healed—to live and testify that trust is not foolishness dressed for disappointment. Faith is not a decorative word people bring out on market days and funerals. Faith is the courage to trust that the Giver of Life can fix anything, arrange anything, reopen anything, redirect anything, if only one has the humility to ask and the patience to trust divine timing rather than personal panic."

Kuma sat on a sun-warmed stone and listened as a breeze passed through dry grass with the hush of pages being turned. "Humans speak often of faith," he said, "but rarely in the same way twice. Some make it sound like membership. Others like technique. Others like noise with uniforms. What do you make of it, Mr. Kuri?"

Kuri gave a slow, almost amused exhale. "From what I've observed, many humans reduce faith to organized religious performance—as though the Infinite were most impressed by scheduling. They count attendance, recitations, garments, postures, and public seriousness, then imagine the matter settled. But faith is larger, deeper, and far more alive than that. Faith is trustful orientation toward the Giver of Life. It is dependence without servility, courage without control, hope without guarantees, obedience without theatrics. It can breathe inside prayer, yes—but also inside service, resilience, stewardship, moral imagination, truth-telling, gratitude, leadership by nurture, repair, and the daily decision not to surrender to despair."

He continued, warming now to the subject in the way only methodical creatures do—thoroughly. "Faith appears in more forms than humans usually grant. It is in the mother who keeps feeding children through drought, the elder who counsels restraint when revenge would be easier, the farmer who plants before certainty of Nature's cooperation, the leader who serves without entitlement, the healer who tends to the suffering without guarantee of thanks, the neighbor who shares water because life outranks ownership, the child who tells the truth while trembling, the community that rebuilds after loss, the conscience that refuses bribery or sellout, the imagination that still expects renewal after ruin. If it moves life toward trust, responsibility, courage, humility, and the common good, faith is already at work, whether or not robes or a choir are present."

Kuri's eyes narrowed kindly. "And those who insist that the One God must be worshipped through only one religious channel often miss the wider splendor of divine complementarity. The Giver of Life created diversity on purpose—not as a theological inconvenience, but as part of what makes existence exciting, meaningful, and relational. Difference need not mean contradiction. Variety need not mean rebellion. Many paths of reverence may still be answered by the same Source when they lead creatures toward truth, humility, justice, mercy, wonder, and care for life. Humans keep trying to hand God a uniform and a mailing address. God, meanwhile, keeps irrigating the whole field."

"Kalingbege the Chameleon told you something important about light, did he not?" Kuri asked. Kuma nodded. Kuri went on. "Light appears colorless only because it holds all colors in full embrace. That is what diversity can produce when it is not feared but welcomed: illumination. When the many are held rightly together, truth becomes more visible, not less. One color alone can be beautiful. All colors together can reveal a world. So it is with peoples, gifts, insights, temperaments, vocations, and forms of reverence. Complementarity is not a compromise of truth. It is often how truth becomes livable."

Kuma smiled. "So, your advice to humans is... what? Pray more? Panic less? Avoid tall trees?"

Kuri looked almost offended by the incompleteness. "Certainly, avoid unnecessary trees," he said. "But more than that: ask. Trust. Wait. Act where you can. Surrender what you cannot. Make room for intervention. Humility is the door through which help enters. Many creatures do not receive because they would rather perform strength than admit need. Yet I tell you this as one descended from a shell shattered into thirteen reasons for despair: the Giver of Life is fully capable of assembling what life has broken, of opening what fear has shut, and of making possible what pride has already declared impossible."

Then Kuri resumed walking with that ancient, uncompromising pace by which tortoises rebuke every species addicted to urgency. Kuma stood and watched him go through the grasses, a small domed testimony moving steadily under the widening Sahel sun. Somewhere on the far end of a branch eavesdropping on the still waters of Venga, Duong's main water source, a weaverbird stitched hanging architecture from stubborn fibers. Somewhere far off, children shouted around a game whose rules were changing mid-play, as usual. From where he stood, Kuma guessed it had to be boys honing their archery skills cross-shooting at the rolled disc carved out of the heavily scarred fleshy bark of the village's largest baobab tree. Arrows handmade by their respective owners with dried out bamboo stems abutted with bicycle spokes secured with special fibers harvested from the shaft of Dawadawa fruits and bound with shea tree sap.

Kuma bowed his head in thanks. Bee had taught him sweetness, butterfly had taught him beauty, bushbaby had taught him humility before interdependence, cat had taught him the ethics of freedom, and now tortoise had taught him that faith was not a narrow corridor guarded by religious gatekeepers, but a vast trustful movement toward the Giver of Life—slow, steady, healing, and broad enough to gather difference into light.

On the seventh day, Kuma rested. He will return soon to the truth quest trail.

About The Author

Constancio Nakuma

Constancio Nakuma is a scholar, educator, and academic leader whose life's journey reflects an uncommon fusion of endurance, learning, and global perspective. Beginning as a weekend herds boy, he rose through determination and study to pursue higher education across three continents: in Accra, Ghana, where he earned his bachelor's degree at the University of Ghana-Legon; in Paris, France, where further study earning him a PhD in linguistics sharpened his intellectual and cultural vision; and in Halifax, Canada, where he completed an MBA that broadened his professional horizons. These experiences formed the foundation of a career devoted to the transformative power of education and the meeting of cultures, ideas, and human possibility. He later served at the University of Colorado Denver as Executive Vice Chancellor for Academic and Student Affairs and Provost, where his leadership was distinguished by a steadfast commitment to academic excellence, student success, and the expansive promise of higher education.

Found in the Wilderness is a visionary novel of quest, reckoning, and renewal. At its center is Kuma, a restless seeker who comes to believe that humanity has strayed from the divine order of creation by refashioning life around conflict, domination, and estrangement from Nature. Drawn into the vast spiritual and ecological landscape of the Sahel, he embarks on an extraordinary journey to recover the wisdom human beings have forsaken. There, through encounters with animals, birds, insects, and reptiles—creatures that have remained faithful to the rhythms and laws of the natural world—Kuma seeks answers to the questions that haunt the human condition: how to live, how to belong, and how to return to harmony with creation. Both philosophical and imaginative, the novel invites readers into a world where wilderness becomes teacher, witness, and mirror. Conceived as the opening volume in a larger series and scheduled for publication in 2026, Found in the Wilderness offers a bold and original meditation on spiritual dislocation, ecological truth, and the redemptive possibilities of listening anew to the living world.

www.ingramcontent.com/pod-product-compliance
Lightning Source LLC
LaVergne TN
LVHW050322160826
845677LV00014B/3511

* 9 7 9 8 9 9 6 3 3 1 2 0 8 *